DUCK DREAMS
CITY BOY TO FARMER BOY

DUCK DREAMS
CITY BOY TO FARMER BOY

by Elizabeth Segel

Towne & Country Press

2013

Book layout by Todd Sanders
Illustrations by Anni Matsick
Printed by CreateSpace

Towne & Country Press
5821 Wayne Rd.
Pittsburgh PA 15206

FIRST EDITION

ISBN: 978-0-6159056-3-1

Part One

1

You want to be **what** when you grow up, nephew?"

"I'm going to be a farmer, Uncle Herman," Simon said firmly. Uncle Herman, Papa's brother and partner in the clothing business, nearly choked on his after-dinner cigar. "What? Who ever heard of a Jewish farmer!" he sputtered. "In the old country, a Jew could maybe own a cow, but not a farm."

"Pa, you're out of date," spoke up Simon's cousin Joe. "Haven't you heard of the 'back to the land' movement? I wouldn't say many Jews are farmers now, but there are a few, I hear. Remember, this is a new world."

"Children, is time to go," Mama called from the kitchen where she was helping Aunt Bella with the washing-up.

"Thanks, Joe," Simon said as he wrapped a warm scarf around his neck, preparing for the brisk walk home with his family.

"You're welcome, cuz, but I'm afraid that if you're set on farming, here in Boston you'll have to settle for pigeon-farming,"

"Ha-ha. Just watch me, Joe," came Simon's voice as he clomped down the stairs.

Simon's dream of becoming a farmer got him into real trouble a few days later. On the first warm day of spring, he sat in mean Miss Kane's classroom as she droned on and on about punctuation. Why didn't the dismissal bell clang? Was it broken?

To pass the time, he pictured himself milking a cow. He could almost hear the swish, swish of milk filling a bucket, when his daydream was interrupted by a fierce whack on his knuckles. "Ow!" he yelled, jumping up and banging his knees on his desk. It was Miss Kane's dreaded ruler. He could barely keep from tearing into Miss Kane, but he stuck his poor knuckles in his mouth and sucked on them instead. He had sworn he'd never talk back to Miss Kane. If he did, she'd be sure to make him stay after school and that was the worst punishment he could imagine.

Miss Kane spoke icily: "Simon Hirsh! I am speaking to you! Answer my question! I cannot understand it. I remember your sister Rachel as one of the best students I have ever taught. You have the brains to be a good student as well. But look at that paper… your diagram looks like chicken-scratching." She screwed up her bony face even more. "You've gotten smudges all over it. Don't your people teach children to wash their hands?"

"Yes, ma'am," Simon murmured meekly, but inside he boiled. Miss Kane thought she was better than her immigrant students and their parents. She was a *real* American, she told them once…as if they weren't! She cracked you with her ruler if you spoke a word of Yiddish or Italian, even if you had just come over from the old country. She even hit Lester Goldberg on the head one day, and Lester couldn't help being slow.

Because Miss Kane's family had been Americans for a long time, that didn't mean that newcomers weren't Americans. Papa and Mama were born in Russia, but they'd gotten their citizen papers in 1900—ten years ago. Simon was only a baby then, but he remembered the year because Papa always said proudly: "Your Mama and I—new Americans for the new American century!"

When the bell rang at last, Simon dashed out, hurrying through the halls to meet his brother Benny at the third-grade classroom. At least it was Friday. No more Miss Kane until Monday.

Benny was watching for him. When they were outside, Simon took off. "Wait for me, Simon. You remember what Mama said," Benny called.

Mostly, Simon did remember. The Boston streets were too crowded and dangerous for his little brother to manage on his own. Mama had said more than once: "Simon, you're the big brother, yes? Be sure to watch out for Benjamin." Even though the brothers were just two years apart, Simon was much taller and faster.

He slowed down and waited for Benny but when they got near the tenement that was home, he started running. He climbed the stairs two at a time, leaving Benny behind. Mama was at the oven, taking out the fragrant braided loaf she'd made for the evening's special Sabbath meal. That was fortunate because she didn't notice that Simon came in alone, but then she turned around and saw Benny arrive, huffing and puffing and glaring at Simon. She set down the challah:

"Simon, Simon, so you can't wait for your little brother? His legs aren't as long as yours," she said as she pulled Benny to her and ruffled his thick dark curls.

"I'm sorry, Mama. I only ran ahead when we were close to home."

Mama shook her head and sighed. "Oh well, for you to be home, boys, is good. Rachel is ready to take baby Sophie out to catch some air. Air you boys also need, yes?" Simon and Benny's job was to take the carriage down the stairs. As they followed Rachel, Mama called after them "Mind your sister now."

Getting down to the street wasn't an easy matter when you lived on the fourth floor of an old tenement. First went Rachel. As the oldest, she carried Sophie, of course. She carefully led them down each dark step and around each landing. The boys' job was to bring down the big wicker baby carriage, Simon in front and Benjamin at the handle. Bump, went the carriage on each step. Bump! Bump! Bump! Past the milk bottles at the Levinson's door, past the smell of the toilet they shared with five other families. Simon thought they would never reach the bottom, but finally he saw the light of the front hallway. Whew! A few more bumps and they were out in the tumult of the city streets.

Even more than usual, on Friday afternoon crowds swarmed the sidewalks. Simon knew that huge boats crammed with immigrants arrived in Boston every week, bringing hundreds of families like theirs to settle into a few city blocks. Peddlers, delivery boys, and housewives jostled each other as they hurried past the shops.

As Rachel buckled the baby into her leather harness, Simon suddenly took off running, unable to be good another minute. "Yah-yah, Benny, you can't catch me!" he yelled over his shoulder, as he dodged around a boy carrying a huge pile of coats on his back. Benny raced after him, darting in front of a knife sharpener's pushcart.

"Boys, wait for me," Rachel yelled as they dashed off. "Simon! Benjamin! You heard what Mama said!"

But Simon kept going. He nearly tripped up a lady loaded with bundles but managed to slip around her by running along the curb, taking care not to step into the street, where huge wagons of every description lumbered by. Simon looked over his shoulder with a grin to see if Benny was following. Just then he glimpsed an ice wagon pulled by an enormous black horse draw over to the curb. At that very moment his brother slipped off the curb and into the gutter. He had fallen under the horse.

"Oh, no!" Simon yelled. "Benny, don't move!"

Benny crouched right under the horse's belly, sobbing and clutching his forehead. By the time Simon got there, blood was trickling through Benny's fingers. Simon wanted to reach under the horse and drag his brother to safety, but the horse shifted nervously from one hoof to another. If he reached for his brother, the horse might step on Benny. Simon couldn't move, remembering Mama telling him that the little bent-over lady in their tenement had been stepped on as a child by a horse.

A crowd gathered as the driver climbed down from the wagon. He shook his head and muttered: "Fool kids… not the horse's fault if a boy tumbles right under him…. gentlest horse in Boston." The ice-man signaled to Benny to stay where he was, then reached up and grabbed the horse's bridle. He stroked its glossy neck. The horse finally stood still, and the driver beckoned Benny to come out.

As Benny slithered out from between the horse's powerful legs, Simon let out a ragged sigh. He felt dizzy and realized he'd been holding his breath the whole time. Rachel crouched beside Benny. She examined the gash over his eye. Simon jiggled the carriage to quiet Sophie who had started to whimper.

Rachel's touch was gentle as she wiped the blood away, but she lit into Simon. "Just wait 'til I tell Mama," she warned. "Benny could have been killed. You are going to get it, Simon!" Simon squirmed and said nothing. What was there to say? Benny would never have fallen under the horse if I hadn't dared him to catch me, he thought.

The driver took an ice pick out of his rubber apron and chipped off a big chunk of ice. "Hold this to your forehead, sonny," he said, offering it to Benny. He didn't seem mad any more. "That'll keep the swelling down, it will. Yer a little soldier, I can see." Simon reached up and stroked the horse's neck. The creature hadn't meant to hurt Benny. He did seem like he wouldn't hurt a fly. Benny too stroked the horse that had frightened him so.

Benny loves animals as much as I do, Simon thought, and sighed. Living in the city, they hardly ever got near an animal.

Rachel picked up baby Sophie and they dragged the carriage back up the stairs to the flat.

2

ack so soon, children?" Mama said, looking up from the potatoes she was peeling, as Simon led a pale and bloody Benny into the kitchen. "Benny!" Mama gasped. Not bothering to wipe her wet hands, she took him in her arms and examined the cut and the big lump on his forehead. "How did this happen, Simon?"

"We were playing tag, Mama, and…"

Rachel broke in, "It was all Simon's fault, and he's older. He should know better. A big horse almost stepped on Benny, Mama!"

Usually Simon would have yelled back at Rachel, but he just said softly: "Rachel's right, Mama. It was my fault." Hanging his head, he listened to Rachel tell the whole story without interrupting her once.

When she finished, Benny murmured, "It was awful scary, Mama, but it wasn't the horse's fault. He was a *nice* horse."

Mama turned to Simon and scolded, "How foolish you act, son. I know you need a place to run and play, but you see what happen when you don't think? I don't know how you …." She broke off and turned away, shaking her head. She took Benny over to the sink and with a damp cloth, gently cleaned the dried blood from under his dark curls. "Gott tsu danken*, at least stitches you won't need."

* If you don't understand a word or words, turn to the Glossary on page 151 for an explanation.

As sundown approached, Simon thought about how hard Papa worked with his brother and cousins, making men's suits and coats and selling them. Papa even had to work Saturdays, the busiest shopping day, so he couldn't be home on the Sabbath except for the Friday night meal. Just then Simon heard footsteps on the stairs that must be Papa's.

"Hello, children, and good Shabbos." Papa kissed Mama, and then it was time to light the candles for the special Sabbath meal, so nothing was said about the accident, though Papa must have wondered about the bandage on Benny's forehead. After the candles were lit, Simon stood in line behind Rachel to feel Papa's hands on his head in blessing.

Soon after he went to bed, Simon heard his parents talking in the next room. He put his ear to the wall, and could hear Mama telling Papa what happened in the street. Before long, though, she slipped into Yiddish, the language of the old country, as she did when she was excited, and Papa answered in Yiddish. Phooey, thought Simon. Because his parents wanted their children to learn English, they spoke Yiddish only to each other, and so Simon couldn't understand what Mama was saying.

Simon had trouble sleeping and woke at dawn. Soon Papa appeared in the doorway and whispered, "I have to get to the store, but we need to have a talk before I go."

"Yes, Papa," said Simon, his heart sinking. He followed Papa.

"Son," Papa began. "Do you understand what a serious mistake you made, encouraging your brother—I might say urging your brother—to take awful chances of being hurt by running into the street?"

"Yes, Papa, I know," Simon said, tears welling up in his eyes. "I didn't mean...I didn't think..."

"I know," said Papa, "but we can take a lesson from this, son. You're not a little child any more. Your brother depends on you to be safe. Can you be someone others can depend on—your brother, for instance? I think you can. Am I right?"

"Yes, Papa," Simon said in a voice so soft that it's a wonder his father heard him. But Papa was saying, "That's my good boy," so he must have heard.

As Papa put on his overcoat, he said: "I'll talk with Mama... We both know you children need fresh air and a place to run around. Perhaps next Sunday we all go to the park for an outing."

3

Simon hoped Mama agreed with that idea. A day outside together would cheer them all up. Sometimes the family took a long walk to a big park in downtown Boston called the Public Gardens. There Simon and Benny could run, play, and shout all they wanted. They could even make friends with a dog or two. Rachel could skip rope and little Sophie could toddle around chasing pigeons. But this outing happened only on Sundays, and not every Sunday.

But on Sunday when the children begged for the outing, Papa shook his head. "Not this time," he said. "Today your mama and I have important business to attend to."

"It's not fair," Simon muttered to Benny. "It's not *fair*," Rachel said to Mama, as she helped brush off Mama's best coat.

"Your Papa is right," said Mama. "I count on you to be my good children." She scooped up baby Sophie to take her to Aunt Bella's flat, so that Rachel could do her homework. She blew a smiling kiss to the three older children, but no one smiled back.

While Rachel did her schoolwork, the boys raced around playing cops and robbers and hollering until Rachel said she couldn't think straight. "I'll make the lunch," she sighed, clearing her books from the table.

After they emptied the steaming bowls of good cabbage soup Mama had left, Rachel said the boys should wash and dry the dishes, since she had gotten the lunch.

"Later," said Simon. "Let's play farm, Benny." He was too old for little kids' pretend play, but there was nothing else to do.

"Really? Sure, Simon," said Benny. He hurried to get out from under the bed the farm set that Papa had bought for them—the red-roofed barn, the little wooden cows and horses, the tiny chickens and ducks. The boys used to play for hours, pretending to be farmers, but today they were soon fighting.

"You had the white horse last time," Simon said as he grabbed it from Benjamin's barnyard.

"No, I didn't! You always have him!" Benny shouted back, and he tried to peel Simon's fingers from around the horse's middle. Soon they were wrestling, rolling around and scattering small animals left and right. By the time Rachel separated them, Simon's lip was bleeding and the pocket of Benny's shirt half ripped off. A cow and a lamb had each lost a leg.

"You can have all the stupid animals," Simon said. "They're only pretend anyway!" Benny sniffled as he gathered up the scattered animals. Simon sighed. He and Benny almost never fought and he didn't even care about the toy animals anymore. Papa said he wasn't a little child any more but he had to admit that he was acting like one.

"Wait 'til Mama and Papa get home…," Rachel said just as they all heard footsteps on the stairs and their parents' voices. Now we're in big trouble, Simon thought. Mama and Papa could see they'd been fighting, and—oh-oh!—the dirty dishes still sat in the sink.

But when Mama and Papa came in they didn't even look at the dirty dishes or the messy floor. They didn't say a word about Simon's lip or Benny's pocket.

"Guess what, children?" said Mama, as she set Sophie down. Papa and I…you'll never guess. We found a house for us."

"A house? For us?" Simon couldn't believe it. He thought only storybook families had a whole house.

Mama went on, "A long time Papa looked. Last month he found a nice house, not too much money. He told me all about it and showed me today… What can I say? We will buy it!" Papa ruffled the boys' hair, hugged Rachel, then swung Sophie up in the air and spun her around. "It's a house away from the city," he said, "a house and a barn and a yard where my boys and girls can run around and breathe lots of fresh air."

That night, Mama came to tuck the boys into their bed, "I didn't want to spoil our wonderful news, sons. But you know better than to fight over toy animals, which is what happened, yes? Simon, you especially need to be sensible. Dangers there are in the country, too, you know. Do you understand?"

"Yes, Mama."

When Mama had kissed them and left, Benny said, "Won't it be great, Simon, to have a house and a yard? Even a *barn!*"

"It sure will," Simon said softly, thinking about what Mama said, vowing to be a better big brother. A moment later, a faint snore told Simon that Benny had fallen asleep, but he lay awake for a long time, thinking about the real animals that they could keep in their real barn. As he drifted off to sleep, he was imagining himself in a henhouse, carefully collecting a basket full of eggs.

4

The next evening, Simon hurried down the street to invite Papa's brother Uncle Herman, along with Aunt Bella and Cousin Joe to come by for a glass of tea. Rachel disappeared in the opposite direction to invite Mama's brother Morris, a kosher butcher, and Aunt Rose, his wife.

Simon raced home after passing along the invitation. "They'll come right over, Mama!" He could hardly wait for the company to arrive. Besides sharing the amazing news, he and Benny loved it whenever Uncle Herman visited. He always put a nickel on the table as they sat down for tea and cake, saying: "There's a nickel for the best-behaved boy. Who will it be?"

With a little brother as quiet and polite as Benny, Simon hardly ever won the nickel, but it didn't matter. As Uncle Herman was leaving, he'd pull a nickel from the ear of whichever boy hadn't won (because he forgot to say please, or interrupted the grown-ups, or knocked over a glass of water). And he somehow made a nickel appear in Rachel's pocket, too.

To make the waiting time go faster, Simon found the tattered farm book that Benny had loved when he was a baby. He pulled Sophie up into his lap and, pointing to each picture, told her the names of all the animals and the sounds they made. "See the cow, Sophie? Cow says 'Moooooo!'"

"Sophie," he whispered, "Do you know we're going to have real animals pretty soon?"

Sophie turned her head to look at her brother. "I like am-mals," she said with a smile and looked back at the book. She caught on quickly and soon chimed in on Simon's "neighs," "baas," and "moo-oo-oos." She kept turning back to her favorite page—the ducks—and quacked away happily until they heard a sharp knock at the door and Uncle Herman, Aunt Bella, and Cousin Joe came in. Uncle Herman sat down without a word to the children. Instead of digging a nickel out of his pocket, he said sternly to Papa: "Now what's this about buying a house, Ezra?"

Papa told them about the house he and Mama were buying away from the city. Mama bustled around, serving the tea and a plate of her delicious apple cake.

"But how will you get to work?" said Uncle Herman, frowning over his fat cigar.

"The streetcar goes all the way from Boston to Melrose now," Papa said. "It will take me the eight miles into North Station—just blocks from the store—and for only ten cents."

"I doubt Melrose has a kosher butcher, Eva, dear," murmured Aunt Bella. Simon shifted in his seat. He hoped Papa and Mama wouldn't change their minds.

"You're right, Bella," said Mama. "I also worried about that. But Ezra says he will get kosher meat from my brother Morris every week and bring it home. We chose Melrose because it has the streetcar line. Out there houses cost not so much money. Also it has lots of space for children to play."

Benny leaned over and whispered to Simon: "When is Uncle Herman going to put a nickel on the table?"

Simon shrugged. Maybe the big news made him forget all about the nickel game.

"But you will be lonely, Eva," Aunt Bella was saying. "All the family is here in Boston. You won't know anyone."

"You will come to visit us, dear Bella," replied Mama. "We want you to take the streetcar to Melrose for Sunday outings."

Simon smiled. He would take Cousin Joe to the barn and show him all the animals they would have. Aunt Bella just shook her head sadly.

The relatives were thinking up more reasons why the new house was a bad idea, Simon could tell. He stopped listening and was trying to get Sophie to laugh at his funny faces when he heard Uncle Herman growl: "Look here, Ezra, will it be safe? Don't you remember what it was like in the old country? …the ruffians who used to come riding through the village to make trouble? Ignorant boors!" he grumbled. "Perhaps there are ruffians in this village."

"Now, Herman, don't frighten the children," Papa said. "That was in the old country. Here I'm sure that if we behave like respectable folk our neighbors will do the same."

Simon wasn't worried about bullies. He knew how to look tough so no one picked on him, or his brother.

"I hope you know what you're doing," Uncle Herman said to Papa, as they got up to leave. "I always say it's your good ideas that have made Hirsh Brothers the fastest-growing clothing business in Boston, but this is one idea if yours I have doubts about."

Simon walked out to the landing with his big cousin. "We're going to have lots of animals on our farm, Joe–probably not a horse, but some chickens, ducks for Sophie, and a cow."

Joe called back, "I don't think your father has plans to go into the farming business. We need him at the clothing store!"

Of course Papa has too much on his mind to think about animals right now, thought Simon as he came back to the flat. Yet surely Papa wouldn't spend good money on a barn and then leave it empty? Simon didn't have long to think about this before two more relatives arrived: Uncle Morris, Mama's brother, and his wife Rose.

Usually when they visited, Aunt Rose talked enough for both of them, and laughed a lot, too. But she wasn't laughing tonight.

They made the same arguments against the move as Papa's relatives had, plus some new ones, but Mama and Papa just smiled. Mama said, "This is another of Ezra's good ideas. You will see."

Simon was getting tired of this. Sure, he'd miss his schoolmates but he'd make new friends. A bigger place would be so much nicer. And Papa said they'd have a toilet in the house, all to themselves. Think of that!

At last Uncle Morris got up and put on his coat. "If it's what you want, sister dear," he said, patting Mama's shoulder.

"That's all very well for you to say, Morris," said Aunt Rose, wiping her eyes. "You'll see Ezra every week when he comes into the store to buy meat. But when will I see my darling Eva? Who will advise me about colic and croup and getting beet stains out of the table linen?" Her tears ran faster. Simon shook his head. How could colic and croup and beet stains be more important than a house of their own?

"Rose, Rose," said Mama, taking her hand. "You'll come out to visit us on Sundays. We're not going to the ends of the earth, you know—just to the end of the streetcar line."

But when they left, Simon saw a tear in Uncle Morris's eye and Aunt Rose sniffled. It was clear that, to them, Melrose might as well be at the ends of the earth.

5

Fortunately, the relatives' arguments didn't discourage Mama and Papa a bit. Still, Simon was disappointed when Mama said: "Of course we can't move until school is over for the year." Oh no, four more weeks of Miss Kane! But finally, that last day of school arrived. When Miss Kane dismissed the class in her chilly way, Simon dashed out, stopped for Benny and they hurried home. Mama had worked hard all week packing up the household goods. Tomorrow would be the big day.

Moving day started with a clip-clop and "Whoa, there," as a big wagon stopped at the curb. Then Cousin Joe arrived to help and he and Papa loaded the wagon with chairs and tables, beds and boxes, while the big horses stood patiently, their long tails swishing to keep the flies off.

Simon was amazed at the heavy mattresses and cupboards his big cousin could carry all by himself. "Show us your muscles, Joe," he said, when his sweat-soaked cousin stopped for a glass of water. Joe rolled up his sleeve and flexed his bicep. Rachel stopped to watch on her way back up for another load of clothes. "Wow," she whispered to Simon, "I bet all the girls are sweet on Cousin Joe."

Simon grinned. He sure didn't want girls "getting sweet" on him, but he did hope he'd be as strong as Joe someday. He tried to pick up Mama's precious sewing machine, but couldn't budge it an inch. Joe would have to load it. He sighed. "Come on, Benny. We've got to help too."

Simon trudged up and down the stairs, with his brother right behind. They hauled armloads of clothes, piles of sheets and towels, and boxes of food. With Benny's help, Simon bumped Sophie's carriage down the long flights of stairs for the last time.

Cousin Joe and Papa appeared in the doorway, carrying the big kitchen table. They loaded it and tied it down, then Joe heaved the sewing machine into the wagon.

"Boys," said Papa. "We have one last task before we leave. We don't want to leave behind the small but important thing that marks every Jewish home."

"Oh, right…the mezuzah," said Simon and as he followed his father back up the long stairs, he thought about those remarkable miniature scrolls on which were written the most holy commandments of the Jewish faith. When they got to the top, Rachel and Mama with Sophie in her arms were on the landing. Papa kissed his fingers and then touched the family's mezuzah on the doorframe of the flat. Pulling a screwdriver from his pocket, he took down the small oblong object. Mama brought a small box from her pocket, put in the mezuzah, and placed it carefully in her handbag. Papa would put the mezuzah up again on the doorframe of their new home.

When they came outside again, the wagon was just pulling out, the driver slapping the horses with the reins and the horses straining against the creaking harness to pull the heavy load.

The family started walking to the streetcar stop while Cousin Joe ran to tell the relatives they were ready to leave. By the time the shiny streetcar pulled up and the family boarded, a crowd had arrived to see them off. Not just Aunt Bella and Uncle Herman, Aunt Rose and Uncle Morris, but five different families of friends and neighbors. The conductor clanged the bell and the streetcar lurched forward. Every one of the ladies except Mama wiped her eyes. Every one of the men looked grave. Mama took out her handkerchief, too, but only to wave a jaunty goodbye to the tearful aunts.

Papa beamed and called: "Come and see us! Now don't forget!"

"Mama," said Simon after they were settled in their seats, "why are all the relatives sad about our moving? We're not going far. Aren't they happy that we'll have our own place?"

Mama's finger touched Simon's cheek gently as the streetcar rattled along. "Simon, dear," began Mama, "saying goodbye to family is hard for us. We can't forget family farewells back in old country. Remember, we all leave parents and grandparents, brothers and sisters. How we sobbed, thinking we maybe never meet again."

Now she was dabbing at her eyes with her handkerchief. "My heart, it almost broke, when my little sister Rifka begged and begged to come. But the journey, it was dangerous and she only a little girl." Mama swallowed hard and went on: "We started out. Little Rifka chased the wagon. When she see she couldn't catch us, she fall down in the road, sobbing." Mama's eyes filled with tears.

"I'm sorry, Mama," Simon murmured and squeezed his mother's hand.

Mama wiped her eyes and shook her head. "We do not let sad memories spoil our new adventure. Don't worry. Since they arrived in Boston, have our relatives stuck their noses outside the neighborhood? No. But you will see. We bring them out to the good country air in Melrose and their worries go away."

At the end of the streetcar line, a horse-drawn carriage and driver waited for them. As they went along, Simon wiggled in his seat and craned his neck, trying to see everything about their new town.

"Sit still, Simon. We'll be there soon, you know" Papa said.

Simon sat still, but pointing to every house they passed, Simon and Benny and even Rachel asked, "Is that it, Papa? Is that our house?" Papa kept shaking his head.

Finally the driver's booming voice called, "Whoa, there!" and his hands pulled hard on the reins. The carriage stopped. The children stared. They saw a white house, a pretty house, with a small red barn in back. Tall trees shaded a big grassy yard. They glimpsed a little brook tumbling along behind the barn.

"Oooh," sighed Rachel. "Papa bought us a park."

6

The next day, as the children unpacked Mama's pots and pans, Simon said: "Rachel, saying this place is a park was silly. It's as pretty as a park, but it's really a farm. We'll get some animals for the barn, and then you'll see."

"It's *not* a farm," said Rachel, sounding like Miss Kane. "We just have a big yard and a little barn. And how can you have a farm without a farmer? Papa will be taking the streetcar to the city every day. He's a tailor, not a farmer." She clanged and banged the pots as she set them on the pantry shelf.

"So what? Benny and me can be the farmers," Simon snapped at his sister. But when, at bedtime, he asked Papa and Mama when they could start getting animals for the barn, Papa laughed and Mama shook her head wearily. "Simon, Simon, what put that idea into your head?"

"Buying this house cost us every bit of our savings," Papa added. "You can run in the yard and splash in the brook, climb the trees and play in the barn. But there's no money for animals. Besides, Mama and I are too busy to take care of animals if we *could* afford them. Now, I want to hear no more about it."

Later in bed, Benny sighed, "Oh well, I saw a dog down the street when we drove through town. Maybe he'll let us pat him."

"Don't give up, Ben," said Simon. "We'll have our farm animals. We just have to start small."

"You mean with a pet mouse, or something?"

"No, silly. Do you remember how Papa said he and his brother and cousins started selling suits from a pushcart until they saved enough money to rent the store? Well, you and I have our savings, don't we?"

"You mean our nickels from Uncle Herman?"

"And don't forget the five dollars we still have from last year's Hanukkah gelt," said Simon. "We can do the same thing. Listen. Here's how we'll persuade Mama and Papa to let us try, Ben. We'll need to do some fast talking but we can do it!"

As Simon shared his thoughts, Benny added his own good ideas. Simon smiled. Mama always said, "Watch out when those two put their heads together." Sure enough, by the time Mama called up "Boys! Time to stop talking," they were ready with their plan.

"But Benny, we'd better not say anything about making a farm for a few days. I think we need to wait until Papa and Mama have settled in and gotten used to this place."

One day the following week, Mr. Avery, the egg man, came around in his delivery wagon. The boys ran out to meet him and kept him talking so long that Mama called out to ask where her eggs were.

At breakfast, Mama set out on the table the blue-and-white milk pitcher that had belonged to her mama. The children poured milk on their steaming oatmeal. Then Mama poured some into a cup for Sophie.

"A family sure drinks a lot of milk," Benny murmured between bites of oatmeal.

"Yep," agreed Simon. "They'd save money if they had a cow. Then they could make their own butter—and cheese, too. Wouldn't have to buy them."

"Simon. Benjamin," said Papa sternly. "We have no money to buy a cow. Now I don't want to hear any more of that foolishness."

"But Papa," Simon pleaded, "We know we can't buy a cow, but Benny and I have been saving up our nickels from Uncle Herman. Hanukkah gelt too. We have almost seven dollars, and we figure that's enough to buy twenty pullets. A pullet—that's a young hen," he explained. "Mr. Avery said we should start with one-month-old pullets. He'll even take us to the farm where he buys his."

Simon was running out of breath, so Benny took over. "You see, Papa, when the pullets grow big, they'll lay eggs. We can sell the eggs and save up to buy a cow."

"Who wants chickens," Rachel broke in, "pecking and scratching all over the yard? Ugh. Nasty things."

"They wouldn't run all over the yard," Simon said. "We can make a chicken house out of the old shed behind the barn."

"If we had a cow, Rachel, we'd get lots of cream," Benny said. "We could make our own ice cream!" The disgusted look on Rachel's face faded. That boy is a genius, Simon thought, trying not to smile. He could tell Rachel was remembering the fun of turning the crank and eating Aunt Rose's delicious peach ice cream.

Papa looked thoughtful, but Mama said, "And who would raise those chicks? I have my hands full with you four chicks, thank you very much. Still…" she paused for a moment, "it certainly would be wonderful to have our own milk and cream."

"We'll take care of the chickens, Mama," both boys said at once. "We'll do everything."

"The egg man will tell us how," Simon added.

"You know," Papa said softly, as he wiped his moustache with his napkin, "I always wanted to be a farmer. My friends used to laugh at me. How could a poor Jew ever own land in the old country? And when I got off the boat in America, I had only twenty dollars in my pocket. I was lucky that my older brother and my cousins made a place for me in their clothing business. But to be a farmer…That was my dream."

"Guess we just take after you, Papa," Benny said, looking angelic. Simon had to choke back a chuckle, but Papa was laughing too! Even Mama was smiling.

"You rascals," Papa whooped. "Your mother is right. Who can hold out when you two set your minds to something?" He raised his eyebrows and looked to Mama. She sighed, then nodded.

"All right, all right," said Papa, tousling the boys' hair. "Build your chicken-house. Buy your pullets. But be prepared to work hard and be patient. It's a long way from month-old pullets to collecting your first egg, and it's even longer from selling your first egg to buying a cow."

7

Before two weeks had passed, the new house felt like home. Simon helped Rachel and Mama unpack the dishes and pots and pans, the towels and sheets, Papa's books and Sophie's toys, while Benny played with Sophie. The next day, after Papa borrowed a cultivator to turn the soil in the garden behind the house, Simon and Benny helped Mama plant a little vegetable garden. But whenever Mama and Papa could spare them, the boys explored the old, musty barn and hay loft, the grassy yard and the apple trees. Across the back of the yard, behind the barn, ran a little brook, with quiet pools and small waterfalls spilling over rocks.

And to think that beyond the brook shone railroad tracks! Simon couldn't believe their good luck. Twice a day, long trains slid clickety-clacking by, already beginning to slow down for the city eight miles away. He liked to run out when he heard the whistle and wave to the engineer as the train glided past. Simon thought their farm was perfect, and Benny agreed. "Aren't you glad there's no school until fall, Benny?" Simon asked. "We can spend the whole summer learning to be farmers!"

For days, Simon worked on turning the falling-down shed into a chicken house. He found an old window frame behind the barn and carefully cut a hole for it in the shed wall. He set up small crates for nesting places and spread straw evenly on the floor.

Papa brought home two rolls of chicken wire and on Sunday helped the boys build a fence. "You don't want your chickens eating up your Mama's vegetable garden," he said. "That would be the end of your chicken farming!"

The next morning Simon gobbled down his oatmeal and stationed himself at the front room window, straining for a glimpse of the egg wagon. Today was the day Mr. Avery, the egg man, had offered to drive him and his brother part way to the farm where they could pick out their very own pullets.

"Here he is!" Simon shouted, and rushed out to the wagon, with Benny close behind. Mama followed with the handkerchief in which she had knotted the boys' precious money.

Mr. Avery handed down Mama's eggs and said: "Well, I guess you'll soon have no need of me, Ma'am, with these up-and-coming young poultry farmers going into the business."

Mama laughed. "I'm sure it will be some time before the boys can supply me with eggs. Besides, what is it they say in America? It doesn't do to count chicks that are still in the shell." She passed the handkerchief up to Simon. "Be careful, boys. Be sure to get healthy birds."

"Yes," said Mr. Avery. "Take your time choosing your pullets, boys. You want healthy ones. I wish I could go with you, but I've got to put in my second planting of corn today."

"We'll do fine," Simon said. He settled himself on the wagon seat beside Mr. Avery and waved to Mama, grabbing Benny with his other arm as the wagon lurched forward. He and Benny would take their time choosing and come home with the best pullets in the flock.

The boys had to walk half a mile from where Mr. Avery turned off to his place, but fortunately a steady breeze cooled the sunny day. Soon Simon saw a rundown farmhouse with lots of chickens running around. No one came when he knocked at the sagging front door, but he heard the whirring sound of a grindstone. Behind the barn they found a rosy-faced man sharpening an axe. He looked up with a frown, but when he heard that the boys wanted to buy twenty pullets, he gave them a big smile. "Pleased to meet you, boys."

He glanced at the lump knotted in Simon's handkerchief and said, "I'd be happy to sell you twenty pullets. Mine are the best chickens in the county." He put down the axe and with his arms around the boys' shoulders, led the way to where a flock of half-grown chicks ran around pecking in the dirt. Simon noticed that the chicken house behind them was half falling down and smelled awful but the pullets looked healthy.

"Ever raised chickens before, young fellas?" the farmer asked.

"No. We just moved here from the city," said Simon, "but Mr. Avery's been telling us how to take care of them."

"We don't want any runty old pullets." Benny spoke up boldly, surprising his brother. "We want the best ones you've got."

"Hey, there's a good one, Simon," he exclaimed, pointing to a bird that energetically flapped its wings, driving another one away from a kernel of corn.

"Right," said Simon. "We'd like that one, please," he told the farmer, "and that one over there."

The farmer's smile broadened. "Certainly, boys. You go right ahead and pick the ones you want. Take as long as you like. I'm in no rush. I'll be looking for crates you can take your pullets home in."

"Gosh, he's a nice man, Ben," said Simon. "I was afraid he'd try to palm off all the runty ones on us."

The boys looked hard at the flock, arguing sometimes over whether a particular chick was good enough. Every time they pointed one out for the farmer to grab, his friendly smile returned. He must be happy to see what good poultry farmers we're going to be, Simon thought. At last, they felt certain they had the twenty biggest and liveliest birds cooped up in the two wooden crates.

The long, sweaty, tiring walk home, carrying the crates, wore the boys out. The constant peeps got on Simon's nerves and he worried that the little feathered pullets might find their way through the slats. But at last they were home with the new arrivals safely in the chicken yard. Simon knew the trip was worth it when Mama and Rachel came out to admire the twenty pecking, flapping, darting birds. Sophie struggled to get down from Mama's arms and began to toddle after one pullet and then another, sending the flock squawking in every direction.

The pullets took to their home with its crates for nests. Each morning Simon filled the upside down bottles with water, and he changed the straw on the floor whenever it got dirty.

The boys could hardly wait to show Mr. Avery their handsome pullets, which grew bigger every day, but for a whole week, Mr. Avery's hired man appeared on the egg wagon. Mr. Avery's rheumatism was acting up, he told Simon.

Finally, one morning as Simon picked Japanese beetles off Mama's bean plants, he looked up and saw the egg wagon coming down the road. "Benny! It's Mr. Avery!" he called, and ran to meet the wagon. While Benny carefully took the eggs in to Mama, Simon led Mr. Avery around the barn to the chicken yard. He stood back proudly and waited for Mr. Avery to speak.

But Mr. Avery didn't speak. Just as Benny joined them, he began to laugh. "Oh, boys, you're not going to get a single egg from *that* bunch. There's nary a hen in the flock. Not one female! They're cockerels!" Catching a look at the boys' faces, he stopped laughing. He rubbed the back of his neck with his big blue bandana.

"I've a mind to thrash that no-good cheat," he growled, "…taking advantage of you boys like that."

Simon and Benny looked at each other. Not a single hen? Not one egg-laying bird? Simon gulped to keep from crying. He blurted out in a shaky voice, "You mean our seven dollars is gone and we did all that work?"

"Don't fret, boys. Cockerels may not lay eggs, but twenty cockerels are nothing to sneeze at. Do you know what I do with my cockerels? I sell them to the Chinese laundryman in town. Then he sells them to a fella who runs a Chinese restaurant in Boston. He takes as many as I can bring him. For your hard work and your seven dollars, you can sell them for—oh, I'd say, twenty dollars. Then you can buy yourselves a dozen *four*-month-old pullets!"

And that is just what they did. Two weeks later Simon packed up their twenty cockerels, and with Benny's help, loaded the crates on their old red wagon. Then they trundled their squawking load all the way to Mr. Lee's laundry. Simon thought he had never heard such a pleasant sound as the twenty silver dollars that clinked in his pocket as they trudged home.

"We can do this, Ben. Give us a little time and we'll have our cow, the prettiest, milkiest cow in America!" He dropped the wagon's handle, grabbed Benny's hands and swung him around. "We're in the chicken farming business, brother!"

8

"What's bothering you, Simon, dear? You're very quiet this morning," Mama asked as she cleared the breakfast table.

"I'm thinking about how hard Papa works. I wish he could be home more."

"I know. I do too. But your Papa, he holds back nothing from whatever he does. He's so grateful to Uncle Herman for taking him into the business that he wants to do everything he can to—how do they call it?—to make Hirsh Brothers a success." She lifted Sophie out of her high chair. "Cheer up, dear, next Wednesday all day long we'll have Papa."

"Truly, Mama?"

"Yes, truly."

"All day long?" Benny added, looking up from his book.

"All day long. Wednesday is July the fourth, America's Independence Day. In the city no one paid attention to this holiday, but this year your Papa is taking the day off from work. He wants to honor the birth of this country with his family and our new neighbors in our new town."

"Hurrah," chorused Simon and Benny. "'Rah," chimed in Sophie.

Simon thought Wednesday would never come, but it came with a bang! He bolted out of bed. Bang! Bang! Pop, pop, pop! His heart thumped until he remembered that today was Independence Day. Some big boys must be setting off firecrackers.

Simon pulled on his clothes. "Come help me feed the chickens, Benny!" he called over his shoulder as he headed for the coop. "I don't want to miss the start of the parade!"

At the breakfast table, Papa asked "Do you understand what makes this day special, children?"

"You don't have to go to work!" Simon and Rachel said at the same time.

"Well, yes. To spend the day with my family is very special. But besides that, this year our family will celebrate with our neighbors the birthday of the wonderful country that drew millions of people like your Mama and me to cross the ocean."

"Yes, Papa," said Simon. Mama and Papa didn't talk much about the old country but he knew that people were very poor there, that a lot of people hated Jews, and that if Papa had stayed, he would have had to be a soldier in the Czar's army for twenty years!

By the time breakfast was cleared away and the family started toward town, people were gathering at the roadsides. "No need to go on further, neighbor," called an old gentleman they recognized from the post office. "This is a good place to stand. They're six deep on the sidewalks in town. Here you'll have front row seats."

"I'm much obliged," Papa answered. "We'll camp right here." Then he pulled from his pocket a fistful of small American flags. "Here, children," he said. "You can wave your flags when the parade goes by."

Papa lifted Sophie up onto a stone hitching post so she would have a better view.

Soon they heard faint marching music. Simon craned his neck to see. After a minute or two, he caught sight of an energetic young drummer and a stoop-shouldered old man carrying a big American flag. "That man fought in the Civil War," the post-office man confided.

The music got louder and louder as the marchers and fancy floats approached. Excited children ran along beside the band, tooting imaginary instruments.

The rest of the morning passed in a blur of excitement. The family followed the crowd to the park in the middle of town. They watched men struggling in a tug-of-war, each side trying to pull the other team into a big pit of mud. They listened to a band concert, while munching on bread and cheese and sweet red strawberries. Simon and Benny started to wrestle.

"Boys!" Mama said. "Be still. Sophie needs her nap now." Sophie was curled up on a blanket, sucking her thumb. With his hat over his eyes, Papa stretched out and dozed too.

Now men were making speeches from the bandstand. Simon didn't want to sit and listen to speeches! He heard excited shouts and squeals from deeper in the park and noticed a crowd of children headed in that direction. "Mama, may we go over to where the games are?"

Mama said yes, and Simon and Benny raced off. Simon saw children pairing up and tying a feed sack over one leg of each child. When he asked the man who was giving out the sacks what they were doing, the man said: "This here's a three-legged race. The finish line is the string between them two trees over there." He looked Simon over. "You're built like a greyhound, boy. Find a partner and see if you can win the prize." He pulled from his pocket two real baseballs. Wow! thought Simon. Maybe he'd try.

He looked around for Benny and didn't find him. Oh well, he could see that you'd never win this kind of race unless you had two kids whose legs were the same length. He wouldn't stand a chance of winning with his little brother as his partner.

Simon looked around. Over to the side, he saw a boy in ragged overalls looking on, all by himself, who was just the right height.

Simon walked over. "Want to race with me?"

The boy looked away, then back. "All right, I guess."

"Good. I'm Simon."

"Patrick here." He ducked his head. "Patrick Keegan."

Simon ran to get a sack and rope and they pulled the scratchy burlap over Simon's left leg and Patrick's right to make one leg. Simon bent over to tie it on with the rough twine the man had given him.

They agreed to start off on the inside leg. The race began. Simon yelped when Patrick crunched down on his foot, and then Patrick yanked so hard he almost fell, but they got the hang of it. Amazingly, the Simon-and-Patrick team got all the way to the finish line without falling (not many teams could say that). They lost out to two bigger boys, but got second prize, two bags of penny candy.

As they pocketed their candy, Patrick mumbled, "Okay, see you around."

Simon wanted to find out more about Patrick but he couldn't think of what to say. "We have twenty pullets," he blurted out. "They're young chickens."

"Can I see them sometime?" Patrick asked.

"Why don't you come tomorrow? I can tell you where we live."

"Oh, I know where you live."

It turned out that Patrick lived on Pleasant Street, also farther out from town, and better yet, he was going to be in sixth grade when school started up again. Simon stood grinning at Patrick. Now he had a friend in Melrose.

"Come meet my folks," said Simon, but Patrick shook his head and slipped away, back toward the field.

Simon headed for his family, then stopped short. Where was Benny? He'd forgotten all about his brother! He couldn't go back without Benny. Simon ran back to the field as fast as he could, wishing he *were* a greyhound. He scanned the clumps of people. What if Benny was lost—scared and crying somewhere? Or he could be hurt again and it would be Simon's fault! But before he could torture himself any more, he saw a familiar dark head over where the horses were hitched.

Benny didn't look a bit upset. He was talking with a tall man who eased a feed bag on an old gray horse hitched to a buggy. They stood in the shade of a huge chestnut tree, out of the sizzling-hot sun.

"Benny!" called Simon. He wanted to bawl Benny out for the scare he'd given him, until he remembered that he had forgotten all about his brother for nearly an hour.

"Hi, Simon," Benny said. "This is Mr. Benton. We've been talking about cows. I told him we're going to buy one someday. He said you have to pay almost forty dollars for a good milker. And, and it costs a lot to feed a cow too."

"That's great, Ben."

"We definitely should get a Jersey cow. Right, Mr. Benton? They're gentle and give rich milk and cream."

"You've got a smart business partner there," the tall farmer said to Simon.

"Yes, sir, I know that for sure. Thank you for your help, sir."

"Ben," he said, as they headed back to the picnic grounds, "I was looking everywhere for you. I'm hot as a cook-stove."

"You sound like Rachel, fussing when we play in the brook too long, Simon."

"It's not funny, Ben," Simon said scowling. He had to be fair though, so he added: "What you found out will be a big help, I have to admit. Now we just have to figure out how to get all that money to buy a cow. Forty dollars. Whew!"

"It's a lot, all right," Benny admitted, looking mournful. Soon, though, he broke out in a big grin. "It may take a long time, Simon, but you know us. When we put our heads together…"

Simon gave his brother a friendly punch and ran ahead to catch up with Papa. He couldn't stay grumpy on a day when he had watched an exciting parade, made a new friend, and when Papa spent this special holiday with them. What a wonderful Fourth of July!

9

"Mama, me and Benny will weed your garden after breakfast. Right, Ben?"

"That will be good help, boys. Thank you."

Simon and Benny gulped down their oatmeal and dashed out. From the garden they could watch for Mr. Avery's wagon, which would be carrying their precious flock of four-month pullets.

"Aren't we lucky that Mr. Avery can't manage all the pullets from his last batch of chicks, Ben?" said Simon. "I'd as soon have a tooth pulled as go back to that mean old farmer again."

He tugged at a stubborn tuft of crabgrass. "Just think, pretty soon we can give Mama all the eggs she needs… *and* have some left over to sell. We'll earn money every week for our buy-a-cow fund!"

"Listen, Simon!" Benny broke in. Yes! Simon heard the clip-clop of the horse's hooves coming closer. The clucks and squawks he heard didn't come from eggs! Mr. Avery drove straight to the chicken yard, the boys running alongside the wagon.

Yesterday, Simon had spent hours cleaning up the chicken coop and spreading fresh straw on the floor. "This is neat as a brass pin," Mr. Avery exclaimed. "Your pullets will be laying twice a day for you in this fancy hotel!" He winked and turned back to the wagon.

Mr. Avery handed down Mama's eggs and then two squawking boxes with white feathers showing through the slats. "Now remember, boys, be sure your birds always have plenty of water. They should do just fine, especially if the weather stays nice and cool. You'll have eggs within the month, I wager." Then with a soft "Gee-up" and a gentle slap of the reins, he was on his way.

After carrying the eggs in for Mama, Benny held each box steady while Simon pried the wooden slats off the top. A dozen pullets tumbled out into the chicken yard and scattered, their nervous squawks turning to contented clucks as they found the feed and water.

"I can't tell your pullets apart," said Rachel, when she came out to inspect the new arrivals. "They all look exactly alike."

"That's okay. They're not pets, you know," Simon said.

"I wish we could have a pet," Benny murmured.

"Me, too," said Rachel. This was news to Simon—good news.

"Maybe later, when Papa and Mama see how well we take care of our hens, they'll let us have a pet," he said. "I figure we'll need a cat to keep the mice from eating the chickens' grain."

"Really?" said Rachel. She smiled as she went back inside to her chores.

The pullets settled into their new home nicely. Rachel complained about the constant cluck-cluck-clucking and occasional raucous quarrels, but Simon loved hearing the sounds of their chicken yard.

He faithfully fed and watered the pullets each morning and evening, and he worked hard to clear out the chicken droppings so the coop wouldn't stink. Benny wasn't much help with that job, but Simon didn't mind doing it. What were a few chicken droppings to a real farmer? He only wished the days would go faster until the hens began laying. He could hardly stand the suspense.

One morning when Simon went out to feed the chickens, the heat felt like midday, and it was only eight o'clock. He had to scamper across the scorching barnyard to keep his bare feet from getting burned.

"You children should stay indoors today," Mama said. She drew the curtains closed to keep the house cool.

"Aw, Mama," Simon groaned. A day in the house? That would be no fun.

"Can we play in the barn, Mama?" he asked. "The barn stays cool." Mama said yes, and so after their chores, Simon and Benny explored the dusty old barn. They climbed the ladder into the hay loft, empty now but still smelling sweet from the old hay. They looked out the haymow door and watched barn swallows swooping back and forth against the brilliant blue sky.

"We have a great old barn, don't we, Benny?" said Simon. "I'll bet every kid we know would give anything to have a barn like this! Seems a waste, though…it being empty all the time."

As the sun climbed higher, even the barn got hot. Simon went to check on the chickens and found the water almost gone, so he filled it a second time. He remembered Mr. Avery saying the pullets would be fine if the weather stayed cool. But what if the weather didn't stay cool?

The hot spell went on for days. Mama saved all the water from cooking and from rinsing clothes and even from the family's weekly baths and poured it carefully over her wilting vegetable garden. "If this goes on much longer, we'll have no tomatoes to put up for the winter," she sighed, "and our melon vines will die."

But it was the pullets that Simon worried about. He filled their water bottle four times a day now, but he could tell they were suffering in the heat. They panted and kept lifting their wings, as if to cool off.

On Sunday, when Papa had time to read the newspaper after supper, he reported that this was the worst heat wave in years. According to the paper, farmers worried that if it didn't break soon, they'd begin losing livestock, as well as seeing crops wither in the fields.

That night Simon had trouble falling asleep. What if the pullets died? Was this try at chicken-farming going to be another failure?

Simon woke up the next morning sweaty and groggy but he headed out to do his chores. Of course, there were no eggs to collect. And when he came in from tending the chickens, he could see that little Sophie wasn't herself. She wouldn't eat her breakfast and didn't want to play.

All that day Sophie was fretful and she wouldn't eat any supper either. Simon woke up in the night and heard Mama hurrying past his door on the way to Sophie's room. He slipped out of bed and followed. Sophie had thrown up in her crib and was shivering in Mama's arms.

"Go back to bed, son. I'm here with your sister."

Simon reluctantly went back to his room, but his baby sister's soft whimpering woke him up several more times. When he did fall asleep, he had bad dreams about Sophie being chased by a big chicken.

The next day was another scorcher, as Papa called it. Sophie just wanted to sit in Mama's lap, holding her doll.

"I think she has a touch of heatstroke," said Mama, wiping the hot little forehead with a damp cloth. "She'll be better soon."

"I hope so," said Simon, groggy from so little sleep. He'd never seen his baby sister sit still for more than a minute.

Simon went out to mix the chickens' mash and fill the water bottle. And as he had every day for a week, he checked each nest while Benny watched. Every nest was empty. He felt like stamping his feet and yelling at these darn chickens but he knew he had to be patient.

"How long will it be, Simon?" Benny complained. "Maybe these birds are cockerels too!"

"Mr. Avery knows a hen from a cockerel. Remember, Papa says farmers have to be patient," Simon replied. But he was getting worried too. Almost a month had passed since the pullets arrived.

The boys hung around the house all day. Simon offered to read the farm animal book to Sophie, but she shook her head. Ben did somersaults to make her laugh, but she just turned away. She hadn't eaten anything and even water came up as soon as it went down.

Sophie finally dropped off to sleep and Mama eased her onto the couch, where she slept for a long time, her damp curls framing her flushed face. The boys played checkers nearby. Mama had just started supper when Simon noticed Sophie stirring. Just as he reached her, she sat up.

"Water," she murmured.

"Want water, Sophie? All right, baby. Simon will get it for you," he said, and ran to the kitchen. He filled a cup with cool water, held it to Sophie's lips, and watched her gulp it down, just as Mama appeared. He held his breath, but the water didn't come right up again.

As he headed out to feed the pullets, Simon thought he heard thunder. Sure enough, big drops of rain began falling. They made a rattling noise on the henhouse roof, as he was putting the fresh straw down. And he could see gusts of wind lashing the maple trees when he looked out the door.

Before heading out into the storm, Simon couldn't resist checking the nests again. Empty, empty, empty. On the fourth nest, a hen sat making little throaty noises. Simon crept his hand gently under her feathers until his fingers felt a smooth something. It was an egg and still warm! "Yes," he crowed, as he pulled out the egg, "you're the winner, little hen!"

The hen gave an annoyed cluck and tried to peck at his hand as she flapped off the nest. Simon held the egg gently and ran back through the deliciously cool rain to the house. "Mama, Benny! Look everyone! We're in the egg business!"

Mama gave him a hug and Benny did too. Rachel said: "I never thought you'd do it, little brothers! Good for you!!"

And Sophie smiled and reached out, saying, "Egg! Egg! Egg for Sophie."

So Mama boiled up that first egg. When it was cooked just right, she chopped up the white and the yellow yoke in Sophie's favorite dish. She sprinkled a bit of salt on it–just the way Sophie liked it. Sophie went right to work with her little spoon and ate it all up.

Simon had never been happier—happy that the heat spell was over and even happier that Sophie was all better. And there was the deep-down happiness of knowing that at last he was truly a farmer.

10

A few nights later, Simon had just climbed into bed when he heard his father coming home. Creeping to the top of the stairs, he heard Papa say, "I have a week's worth of kosher meat and exciting news."

Papa looked up and beckoned Simon down.

"What is this exciting news, Ezra?" asked Mama.

"On Sunday, Uncle Morris and Aunt Rose, Uncle Herman, Aunt Bella, and Cousin Joe all will come out from the city to visit us."

"Oh boy," said Simon. "Wait 'til they see our chickens!"

Mama only murmured "At last! Oh, Ezra, I'm so pleased." Though Papa looked gray with tiredness, he took Mama in his arms and danced her around. Simon had been so busy with the chickens, he hadn't thought about how Mama must miss having the relatives visit, like they did back in Boston.

For the rest of the week, Mama bustled about, cleaning and polishing. Simon made sure the chickens had clean straw and weeded four rows of Mama's beets and carrots. Rachel ironed the best linen napkins. Benny helped by keeping Sophie happy and out of everyone's way.

That Friday evening, before Shabbat began, Simon helped Papa make a horseshoe pitch, using a couple of railroad spikes the boys had found and horseshoes that someone had nailed up over the barn door.

When Sunday came, Simon went with Benny and Rachel to the streetcar stop. "Here it comes," shouted Simon, when he heard the faint ringing of the trolley's bell. In no time the trolley arrived and Cousin Joe helped the aunts down to the street.

The relatives were all dressed up. The uncles wore straw hats instead of their usual caps, and the aunts' wide hats, trimmed with flowers, set off their long sweeping dresses of pretty sprigged calico.

The aunts tried to hug each child in turn but Simon escaped. While the uncles ruffled Benny's hair and tweaked Rachel's braids, he started for home. "Follow me, everyone, to our new place!"

"Enough of this kissing and cooing. Let's go!" agreed Cousin Joe, "I want to see this wonderful house and barn."

"And chicken coop! Don't forget the chicken coop," said Simon.

When they reached the front porch where Mama, Papa, and Sophie waited, the grown-ups kissed Sophie and pinched her chubby cheeks until she buried her face in Mama's shoulder. Then they wanted to explore every room of the house. Simon thought they'd never finish exclaiming about the new stove, the spacious pantry, and the four nice bedrooms.

At last they came out to stroll around the yard.

"Come on, everyone," Simon urged. "Come see our chickens."

"I'm sure they're very nice, dear," said Aunt Rose, "but I don't think…" Her voice trailed off as she tugged on Uncle Morris's arm to return to the house. Aunt Bella was already headed that way. Simon couldn't believe it. No one wanted to see the chickens? He blinked and swallowed hard.

"Oh, come on, dear," said Uncle Morris. "Let's just take a quick look at the pullets. We don't want to disappoint the boys." He took Aunt Rose's hand firmly and stepped through the opening in the chicken-wire fence into the flock of pullets, busy running after bugs or pecking at their feed.

Simon led Uncle Morris into the chicken coop itself. Uncle Morris ducked going through the low door, but Aunt Rose, pulled along behind, hit her head. Her beautiful hat flew off and landed in the straw. Then she stumbled over a pullet. The bird squawked and flew up right by her head. Aunt Rose let out a shriek that hurt Simon's ears. In her rush to get out of the chicken yard and away from the birds, she caught her beautiful dress on the chicken wire fence. Rrrrip! Simon heard. Oh, no!

Under the elm tree, Uncle Morris stood holding Aunt Rose, trying to calm her with pats and kisses. "There, there, Rosie," he murmured. "No harm done."

"No harm done!" sniffled Aunt Rose. She bent over to finger the tear in her dress and discovered a mass of cobwebs swept up by the hem of her dress. "My new dress…" she began to cry again.

"Rachel, get Mama!" Simon called, and in no time, Mama came out and hurried across the yard. "Oh, my poor Rose," she said and gathered Aunt Rose in her arms. She surveyed the damage. "Now don't you worry. We'll brush you off and then I can mend that rip in no time. You'll never know it was there, I guarantee." She guided sniffling Aunt Rose to the house.

Simon felt awful. The special day was ruined. Mama and Papa would be so disappointed.

"Come on, boys," said Joe. "I'm not afraid of cobwebs and chicken wire. Let's see those wonderful birds of yours." Good old cousin Joe, thought Simon. With his straw hat under his arm, Joe ducked into the chicken coop. He counted the pullets and admired the roosts. "And how about eggs?" he asked. "Are your hens earning their feed yet, boys?"

"Six or seven eggs every day this week," Simon said, and showed Joe the neat chart Benny had made to record each day's egg count.

"Charting your production? Good for you, cousins," Joe said, clapping them both on the back. "You boys will make good businessmen as well as good farmers."

"Benny had the chart idea," Simon said. "He's the businessman here."

When Joe and the boys emerged from the chicken yard, the men were rolling up their sleeves to begin a game of horseshoes. Simon peeked in the back door. Aunt Rose had joined the ladies shelling peas. Whew! She must be feeling better.

He dashed over towards the horseshoe pitch, where he could hear the clang of horseshoes striking the stake and the men's groans and cheers. Joe had joined the contest. Simon and Benny cheered him on. Simon cheered for Papa, too, and was proud when Papa's horseshoe circled the stake cleanly to win the match.

Then came the clang, clang of the dinner bell. Wiping their moist foreheads with big white handkerchiefs, the men led the way back to the house.

The dinner table, extended to its full length, held heaping plates of Mama's good food: roast chicken, home-grown peas, pickles, crusty bread, and much more. Simon's mouth watered just to look at it.

And there was Uncle Herman, fishing a nickel out of his pocket and putting it on the table with a flourish and a wink at the boys. Simon nudged Benny and grinned.

The hubbub of conversation died down as people attacked their full plates, with someone occasionally murmuring about the delicious food.

When everyone had had seconds, Uncle Morris turned to Joe. "Well, young man, what news? It's time you were looking for a wife, isn't it?"

Joe mopping up the last of the gravy with a crust of bread replied, "Hey! What's the rush? I'm in no hurry."

"Tell them about the young lady you took to the Yiddish theater last week, Joe," said Papa.

"Well," said Joe, "to start with, when I came to pick her up, I walked smack into a crowd of her relatives. They had gathered to look me over, I guess. Besides her parents, there were three uncles lined up. One even asked me if I make a good living." He sighed and pushed back from the table.

"And then," he went on, "the young woman didn't like the show—said she was too tired. When she told me on the way home that bending over gives her headaches, so I shouldn't expect her to dust under the beds.... well, I almost left her right then and there to walk home by herself."

Simon giggled. Papa and the uncles were laughing so hard that tears ran down their cheeks. "Headaches, is it?" sputtered Uncle Herman.

"I didn't mind the headaches as much as her thinking she'd be cleaning under my bed just because I'd asked her out once," Joe explained. "No, I think I'll stay a bachelor for a while longer."

After three strawberry pies disappeared, the ladies gathered up their shawls and bags and the men their straw hats to catch the streetcar back to the city. Uncle Herman gave Benny the nickel from the table ("I saw that boarding-house reach, Simon, my boy"), at the same time drawing another from Simon's ear.

"My hat!" cried Aunt Rose. "My beautiful new hat! It must still be in the chicken-coop."

"We'll get it," cried Simon and Benny at the same instant. As they raced out to the chicken yard, Benny said: "What if it's ruined? The relatives will never come back."

"We'll have to buy her a new one, that's all," said Simon. In his mind, he saw their precious egg money melt away.

When Simon spotted the hat, his worst fears seemed true. The hat was lying in a corner, upside down on the floor, with a pullet firmly settled in her comfortable new nest.

"Shoo, shoo," scolded Simon, tipping the hat and dumping the pullet out. The pullet scolded back as she fluttered over to the packing-crate nests.

Simon held his breath as he checked the hat for damage. Thank heaven the pullet hadn't laid an egg in it! Together the boys picked out downy pullet feathers and loose straw. Simon smoothed out the ribbons and gave the hat a final brushing. "Good as new," he declared, and both boys sighed with relief.

Benny grinned as Simon presented Aunt Rose's precious hat with a flourish. "Thank you, boys," she said, and gave each of them a kiss. "Next time we won't dress up, so we can explore every nook and cranny of this beautiful place." She settled the hat firmly on her head and secured it with a long hatpin. Everyone began exchanging good-bye hugs and kisses.

"Come back often," Mama called after the aunts and uncles, as they started out.

"Don't worry, we will," several voices cried. Then came Uncle Morris' deep voice: "I'd travel a hundred miles for Eva's strawberry pie."

After the dishes were washed and dried, the family sat on the porch, tired but happy. Mama fanned herself and the only sound was the rhythm of the rocking chair and the quiet snuffles of Sophie's thumb-sucking, as she nestled in Mama's arms. Everyone was startled when a familiar voice called out of the dusk, "How are my chickens coming along?"

11

Mr. Avery stepped out of the shadows. He had changed his overalls and muddy work boots for his Sunday best. Simon hardly would have recognized him, except for his beaming smile and friendly voice.

Mama introduced Mr. Avery to Papa and invited him onto the porch. Then she went to fetch him a glass of cold lemonade.

"Glad to meet you, Mr. Hirsh. I was worried about the boys' pullets during that there heat spell we had. I knew how hard they worked to get started. It would have been a gol-danged shame if any of their birds died in the heat." Simon looked at Papa, but Papa didn't take any notice of Mr. Avery's colorful word.

"The pullets suffered some, I think," said Simon, "but we lost nary a one."

"Well, that's a relief to me. Boys, are your pullets laying yet?"

"The pullets are laying like a house afire, Mr. Avery. I found seven eggs yesterday, eight on Friday."

"Well, I'll be jiggered," said Mr. Avery. "Your hens will be the talk of the county." He sat down carefully, with his Sunday hat on his lap.

Papa thanked Mr. Avery for all the help he'd given the boys. "I'm no farmer, you see, and without your advice, we wouldn't have an egg for Sophie's breakfast every day and more besides."

That reminded Simon that he had to see that the chickens were safe for the night. He hurried through his chores so he wouldn't miss anything. As he came back around the corner of the porch, he heard Mr. Avery say, "There's something I wanted to tell the up-and-coming poultry farmers. Mr. Lee is in the market for ducks for his friend's Chinese restaurant. With their pullets doing well, I thought the boys might like to try their hand at ducks. I brought this here farm bureau pamphlet–explains all about raising ducks."

Simon bounded up the steps as Mr. Avery set the pamphlet on the railing. He was disappointed to hear Papa say firmly: "I think the boys have their hands full with the pullets, Mr. Avery. But thank you very much."

"I understand. Just thought I'd mention it. Ducks are very little trouble and bring a nice profit." He turned to Simon. "How many eggs tonight, Simon?"

"Just five, I'm afraid. We had a little excitement in the chicken coop today, with all our visitors. Probably it got the pullets stirred up."

"Ah, yes. You'll have your ups and downs, boys, but sounds like your flock is flourishing. Your hard work is bound to pay off."

Mr. Avery got up to go and Papa walked him to his wagon, thanking him again for taking an interest in his boys.

Mama shooed the boys off to bed. "Aw, Mama," complained Simon.

"I'll be right behind you. Standing up, I could fall asleep after a day like this!"

As they undressed, Simon pulled something from his pocket. It was the pamphlet Mr. Avery had brought: *Raising Ducks on the Small Farm*. "Ducks, Benny! Think of that!"

"But Papa said we have our hands full, Simon."

"I heard," said Simon. "But ducks are 'very little trouble and bring a nice profit,' you know." He grinned and Benny smiled back, shaking his head.

Benny was fast asleep before Simon put down the pamphlet and blew out the lamp, his head full of duck farming ideas.

Again the next night, Simon kept the lamp burning long after he and Benny had "climbed wooden hill," as Papa put it. The more he read about keeping ducks, the more excited he became. He just had to figure out a way to persuade Mama and Papa to let him buy some ducklings.

In the morning, Mama left to do her grocery shopping. Simon begged a piece of paper from Rachel, who was filling a page in her notebook with sketches of cats. He settled down at the kitchen table. Writing as neatly as he could, he began to prepare a list of reasons why he and Benny should keep a flock of ducks. He didn't copy the big words of the pamphlet. Mama's English wasn't quite as good as Papa's, who had studied English in the old country.

"Ducks are energetic foragers," said the pamphlet. The meaning of this escaped Simon at first, but then he understood. *Ducks can find a lot of their own food. They eat bugs and slugs and weed seeds,*" he wrote as reason number one. Mama would welcome the ducks' help with ridding her garden of pests and weeds, he was sure.

He looked at the pamphlet again and then wrote: "Reason #2: *Ducks produce down and feathers that make excellent pillows.*" Another good argument for Mama.

"*Ducks do well even in cold or hot weather,*" Simon wrote as reason #3. Mama and Papa could see how that would save a ton of worrying.

Now what was this strange word "manure"? Oh yes, Simon remembered now. "*#4: Duck poop makes an excellent fertilizer.*" Mama had paid Mr. Avery for a load of fertilizer last spring for her garden. She'd be glad to have free fertilizer. He thought for a minute, then he erased "poop" and squeezed "manure" into the space. This had to be grown-up sounding, business-like.

Simon went back to the pamphlet for his next reason and read: "Ducks can be noisy and for that reason are not enjoyed by some people." Simon decided not to mention that. He would make sure his ducks had plenty of food and water, so they'd have nothing to quack about.

The clincher, Simon was sure, was reason #5: *"Ducks can grow from newborn ducklings to seven-pound birds in just ten weeks!"* If they bought their ducklings soon, the birds would be ready to sell at a nice profit before winter set in!

Simon smiled and went to look for Benny. He found him curled up in Papa's chair, reading another Rover Boys story. Simon gave him the paper with a flourish.

"You did a good job," Benny said, after reading the list. "Just be ready for all the reasons Mama and Papa will have for *not* getting ducks."

"But…" Simon said with a grin, "we can always remind them that 'Ducks are very little trouble…'"

"'…and bring a nice profit.' I know. Good luck, brother. You'll need it."

The next night after Mama put Sophie to bed, they all sat on the front porch, except for Papa, who hadn't gotten home from work. Mama would be the one to convince anyway, as the ducks would make extra work for her. Simon looked at Benny, took a deep breath, and began.

As Simon made his case for adding a flock of ducks to their little farm, Mama listened silently. That was a good sign. She nodded when he listed all the things ducks would contribute to the family. When he had finished, Simon held his breath. At last Mama said, "Have you thought where you will keep these ducks, Simon?"

"We'd keep them in the barn at first—for three weeks. Then we'll make a pen beside the barn. When they get bigger, they can wander around. Except at night…they'd be in the barn at night, safe from foxes."

"We'll need a barn cat to protect them from rats," he went on, "but Rachel wants a cat. Right, Rachel? A barn cat is no trouble, Mama."

"And your ducks wouldn't fly away?"

"We'll get the kind that can't fly. The pamphlet Mr. Avery left tells all about what breed of ducks we need, and how to take care of them."

"Mama," Benny broke in, "We can get three-week-old ducklings for only five cents each. Then Mr. Lee's friend will buy them in just ten weeks for fourteen cents a pound, Mr. Avery said. And they should weigh seven pounds by then!"

"It won't cost much to feed them, Mama," Simon added, "chicken feed with brewer's yeast from the feed store at first. Then they'll eat table scraps and weeds and bugs."

"I see," Mama nodded. "You've learned a lot about ducks, I can see."

This was going well, Simon thought. Rachel was staying out of it because she might get her cat at last. "Don't you see, Mama," Simon got to the most important point: "we'd be helping out. Then Papa won't need to work so hard. And it would be good practice. Benny and me…" He paused and corrected himself, thinking of Miss Kane's knuckle-rappings. "Benny and *I* want to be farmers when we grow up, right, Ben?"

Benny squirmed in his chair. A blush spread across his face. Come on, Ben, Simon thought. Don't get tongue-tied on me! Mama's going to say yes. I'm sure she is.

"Simon," Benny said softly, "You want to be a farmer. I like helping you, but I don't know…" his voice trailed off. "I love animals, but I don't really want to be a farmer when I grow up," he said in a whisper.

Simon stared at his brother, his partner. He couldn't have been more surprised if Benny had said he was running off to join the circus.

"I want to work with Papa in the clothing business," Benny explained, his eyes pleading with Simon to understand.

Simon saw Mama beaming at Benny. "Benny, Papa will be so pleased and proud to hear that."

Simon fought back the tears that were about to spill over. He sat down hard on the front steps with his back to the family.

After a moment, Benny came over and sat beside him. He put his arm around Simon's shoulder. "I'll still help. A good farm is a business, right? I can help with the money part. I just don't want to raise animals and crops when I'm grown up. You're the one who's good at that."

Simon didn't speak. His dream of farming with Benny was ruined. And his duck argument was off the tracks.

But Mama was speaking quietly. Simon heard her say, "I notice how hard you boys have been working–you especially, Simon. Your Mama knows you need to be busy…busy helps you stay out of trouble.

Your Papa and I have talked about this. We think your farming—it's a good thing."

"We do," Papa replied, as he came up the walk. "You made a nice profit on your cockerels, boys, and now the egg money helps with the housekeeping expenses. You're on your way to being good farmers *and* good businessmen."

Mama explained to Papa: "Simon wants to try raising ducks. He's thought it through, I think."

"I was afraid it might be too much," Papa said, "but if you think so, Eva."

Mama nodded and turned back to Simon. "Listen to me, son. Your main job in the fall will be schoolwork. We will say yes to the ducks, but if you don't do well in your studies, or if you get into trouble at your new school, fttt!" She tossed her hand in the air. "Like that, the ducks *and* the chickens will have to go. Do you understand?"

Simon turned and faced Mama. He felt like his brain couldn't keep up with his ears. Mama was saying yes! He stammered out, "Yes, Mama. I understand. I know I can stay out of trouble."

Mama sipped at her tea. Simon sat on the porch steps trying to sort out a jumble of thoughts. He heard Rachel and Benny say good night and start upstairs.

"And now to bed with you, Farmer Simon," said Papa. "Your chickens will be up with the sun and so will you, I know."

Simon gave his Papa a fierce hug. He turned to Mama and hugged her too. "Thank you, Mama. I won't disappoint you. I promise." She took his face in her hands and kissed his forehead. "That's my good boy," she murmured. "Sweet dreams, son."

"Duck dreams tonight, I'll wager," said Papa with a smile.

12

Just four days later, the family watched as a flock of three-week-old ducklings took over the barn. They poked their bills into the feed and water troughs that Simon had found in an old stall. They foraged for bugs in the corners. A few busily groomed the new white feathers that were replacing their down.

"Duckies, duckies!" Sophie exclaimed.

"Mustn't touch, Sophie," Mama said, holding firmly to her hand.

"Pat ducks," Sophie said. "Sophie be gentle."

"No, Sophie," said Simon. "No patting ducks. Not even Simon can touch the ducks today. The ducks need to get used to their new home."

Sophie was determined, so Rachel took her out to pat the handsome new barn cat that sat preening in the sunshine. "Thanks, Rachel," Simon said.

Rachel had found the cat on her own, asking around the neighborhood if anyone had a cat to spare. Two houses down the street she found this pretty half-grown gray cat, the last of a recent litter. She named her Elizabeth Eliza after a character in a book she liked. Simon thought that was a ridiculous name, but he didn't tease her. After all, she had stopped turning her nose up at his farming ideas.

After Mama and Papa went inside, Simon and Benny sat on an old wheelbarrow and watched the new residents of their farm waddle around. The ducks made funny noises as they went about their business, quiet throaty quackings. Good, Simon thought, remembering the pamphlet's caution about Pekin ducks being noisy. I guess I don't have to worry about these ducks disturbing anyone.

"This is really beginning to feel like a farm, Benny, don't you think? Chickens in the chicken coop, ducks in the barn, and a real barn cat to keep the mice and rats from eating the grain."

"It *is* a farm, Simon. We need to give it a name. We could call it Brook Farm 'cause we have a brook."

"That's too plain."

"How about Sunnybrook Farm?" said Rachel, who appeared in the barn door, carrying the cat. "Last year my teacher read a book to us about a Sunnybrook Farm."

"Sunnybrook Farm's a good name for a farm in a book, Rachel," said Simon. "But it sounds too... too sweet for a real farm. I know! Let's call our farm 'Roaring Brook Farm.'"

"Roaring brook!" scoffed Rachel. That brook's about a foot deep and as gentle as a lamb. It's no roaring brook!"

"Roaring brook sounds better, right, Benny?"

"Right."

"Oh, I don't care anyway," Rachel said, heading for the house. "It's not a farm either. Just saying that doesn't make it one, you know."

"Girls," grumbled Simon, shaking his head. "All right. Roaring Brook Farm. It's settled then. Now it's time we got back to work on the duck pen, Benny."

Papa had already helped by sinking two posts, but the rest was up to Simon and Benny. Simon brought out the leftover chicken wire fence and they began the big job of stringing it between the barn and the two corner posts.

It was hot, slow work, so Simon was glad to see Patrick coming down the road. "Hey, Patrick! Come see our ducks," he shouted. He and Patrick had seen each other around, but Patrick was always too busy doing errands for his mother to come over. But this time Patrick turned into the yard.

"Let me have that hammer," Patrick said to Benny. "You hold the wire in place and I'll pound." Benny turned over the hammer without a murmur. He had hit his thumb more often than he hit the big staples they were using to secure the fencing. With Patrick's help, the job went quickly and by the time the 4:15 train glided by, the pen was ready for the ducks.

"Thanks, Patrick," said Simon. "This will keep the ducks safe. Next week they'll be old enough to wander around in daytime but they'll still need to be in here at night."

"Where are your ducks going to swim?" asked Patrick.

"The book says these ducks don't need to swim," Simon said. "They're happier if they have a swimming place but they don't need one."

Patrick shrugged and began to help Simon roll up the unused fencing and carry it to the barn.

"How'd you like to come exploring with me?" Patrick asked.

"Exploring? Where?"

"At the town dump. You'd be surprised what you can find that folks have thrown away."

"Okay. Come in while I ask Mama."

They found Mama shelling new peas. Patrick hung back, looking at the floor.

"Mama, this is my friend Patrick."

"It's good to meet you, Patrick," Mama replied, "Simon's three-legged race friend, right?"

"Yes, ma'am."

"Mama, may I go exploring with Patrick? Please?" Simon asked. He wasn't sure his mother would like the idea of exploring the town dump, so he didn't mention it.

"To have a good time is a fine idea after all that work. But don't go far, boys," she said, "and be back by suppertime, Simon."

After they were out of earshot, Patrick said. "Your mum's nice. You know, most mothers don't want their kids 'sociating with shanty Irish."

"What does shanty Irish mean?"

"It means everyone looks down on us because we're poor. Most of the Irish, like my folks, were dirt-poor when they came here. My father works hard at the rubber shoe factory, but even though the work is dangerous, he gets only six dollars a week, and we have lots of kids…"

"How many? Simon asked.

"Seven, aside from three that died when they were little babies," Patrick answered.

Simon murmured, "Gosh, Patrick," but Patrick plowed on.

"My father says he's lucky to have a job at all. Most signs announcing jobs say 'No Irish.'"

Simon understood. Papa had told him they were lucky the last owner of Roaring Brook Farm sold it to them. A lot of people wouldn't sell a house to a Jew. But Simon didn't say anything about that. It sounded like Patrick's family was much worse off.

Patrick led the way up a rutted dirt track. Good thing the dump wasn't too far away, Simon thought, since he had promised Mama to be home for dinner. He could smell smoke. A pile of rubbish smoldered down in a hollow. He saw junk scattered all around: broken crockery, the skeleton of a baby carriage, a hay rake with missing teeth, a rusted-out parlor stove. The smell of rotting garbage mixed with the smoke.

Patrick yanked a chair with a broken leg from underneath an old wagon bed. "Ain't it amazing what folks throw away? I can fix this up just fine and then Maureen—she's the littlest besides the twins—she won't have to sit on a box at the kitchen table."

Simon poked around in a pile of trash and pulled on something heavy, trying to figure out what it was. "Hey, Patrick!" he called, "Look what I found! Help me pull it out."

"An old tin tub! What do you want that for? You folks need a bathtub?"

"Nope. We've got a bathtub, but you gave me an idea back there. You see before you a private little swimming pool for the newest residents of

Roaring Brook Farm. Talk about throwing out things that are good as new! What do you think?"

"I think that's a poor excuse for a duck pond."

"Aw, you're just jealous that you didn't think of it yourself." Simon walked around the tub, as pleased as if someone had handed him a dollar. "Whooee! Just wait until those little quackers see what I have for them!"

13

"Hey, Pat! Help me get this thing out from under these rusty old pipes," Simon grunted. Patrick pushed and Simon pulled on the old tin bathtub until it was free.

"Look! It even has a plug in the drain! All we need to do is dig a hole for it."

"I don't know," said Patrick, shaking his head. "You've got twelve ducks, Simon. They'll never fit in this thing."

"They can take turns. The ducks will love it. Can't you just see the little quackers paddling around in this?"

Simon walked all around the tub, admiring his find. A few dents and some half-rotted oak leaves in the bottom didn't matter.

"Besides, getting this to your place is going to be a heck of a job," Patrick grumbled. Simon could see he was right. The tub wasn't that heavy, but it was big and awkward. "We'll be stumbling all the way back to the farm, trying to carry it and see where we're going."

"We can do it, Patrick. We'll just have to rest every little while." But then he'd be late for dinner, he realized. Drat!

"Wait a minute!" Simon dashed off to one of the piles of junk. He was back in two minutes, pushing the skeleton baby carriage. "The wheels are still good on this broken-down old thing! We can wheel the tub home on them. Come on, Pat. Don't let me down."

"Okay, okay. Just don't expect me to do any digging. I can't fool around like you can on some crazy scheme. I've got to take care of the little ones tomorrow. My Mum and big sister got a job cleaning some rich lady's house."

"That's okay, I can do it," Simon said, as they struggled to lift the tub onto the carriage frame. Patrick put the broken chair he'd found in the tub and they began trudging silently down the rutted track.

The trip was slow going. The wheels squeaked horribly, and the tub rocked from side to side, needing to be steadied by one boy while the other pulled. Finally they were on the last downhill stretch to Roaring Brook Farm.

Patrick stopped short before they reached the bottom. "You can make it from here. I got to get home." He grabbed the broken chair and sprinted back up the road. "Shoot," Simon muttered. He had all he could do to keep the tub on the carriage as he maneuvered into the yard.

Rachel was clearing away the plates. "Simon," said Mama. "I can't believe you disobeyed me and missed one of the few meals of the week with your Papa."

"I'm sorry, Mama. We lost track of time," he mumbled.

"And just what were you doing that was so interesting?" asked Papa. Simon explained about the tub he found at the dump and how great it would be for the ducks. Mama said nothing as she served him his cold dinner. No one seemed excited by his plan, and Papa made him promise to be on time for meals in the future.

"And Simon," Mama added, "I don't want you go to that dump again. Too many rats and germs in such a place…"

"Yes, Mama," sighed Simon, scooping up a spoonful of stone-cold peas. "I hope I wasn't wrong about your friend, Simon. He has a nice polite way about him, but if he's allowed to run wild he may not be good…what is the word? … a good influence."

"Patrick's okay, Mama. Bringing back the tub was my idea."

The next day was what the old-timers called "a scorcher," but Simon wanted to get started. He found the long-handled shovel and began digging. He had to start over after he hit the root of the big maple tree. The shovel felt heavier and heavier and blisters on his hand got bigger and bigger. After a few more minutes, the blisters popped and oozed. That made the digging even harder.

"You're getting awful red in the face, Simon," said Benny, who had come to watch. "Why don't you rest? I can dig awhile."

"Are you kidding? You're not strong enough for this kind of work."

Benny looked as if Simon had slapped him. Simon glanced away. Benny always hated being reminded that he couldn't do everything his big brother could.

Benny blurted out, "It's just like Mama says, Simon. Sometimes you don't think straight. You've told me a hundred times how fast our ducks will grow. How can they swim in this little bitty tub?"

Little bitty tub, thought Simon. Little bitty tub! If you were doing the digging, smart guy, you'd know this thing's enormous. "Drat it all, anyway!" he grunted, heaving a shovelful of dirt over his shoulder. "You're as bad as the rest of this family. Nobody around here has a speck of imagination."

The next time he looked up, Benny was nowhere in sight. Simon bent to carve out another shovelful of heavy dirt. Only the thought of seeing his ducks paddling in the tub kept him going. He had never worked so hard in his life.

Finally, Simon finished the hole and yelled for Benny. Much as he hated to admit it, he couldn't get the tub to the hole and sink it without help. Benny appeared with a pail of water and a dipper, which he silently handed to Simon. Simon drank four dipperfuls. "Thanks," he muttered, putting the dipper back in the pail. He felt bad about being mean to Benny, but not bad enough to apologize.

"Can you help me get the tub in, Benny?"

"I guess," said Benny, shrugging his shoulders. They worked without speaking, wheeling the wobbly tub to the hole and wrestling it in. Then Benny went back into the house. Looks like he's still mad, Simon thought.

All right, this is my idea and I'll finish it myself. He found some putty in the barn and used it to seal the plug in the bottom of the tub. To fill it to the brim took him twenty sweaty, staggering trips from the kitchen with heavy pails of water. He went in to wash up for dinner thinking he'd show them all that this was one of his best ideas ever.

14

After dinner, Simon went out to the barn. The half-grown ducks greedily attacked the carrot and potato peelings Mama had saved for them. Simon opened the door from the barn to the duck yard, then went in and carried out the nearest duck. The others came waddling after.

At first, being outdoors stirred up the ducks so much that they ignored the tub. They explored the fence; they snapped up bugs from the grass; they waddled about importantly, quacking all the while. Finally, a bold duckling stood at the edge of the tub and stuck his bill into the water. In an instant, he slipped into the tub and began paddling vigorously.

"Hey, Benny, come see our ducks!" Benny came out carrying his book, and behind him appeared Rachel with Sophie. Mama even left the dishwashing to watch.

"Look at that one, Simon! He's taking to his new pool like… like a duck to water!" Benny cried.

"Yep. Whoever thought up that saying knew what he was talking about," Simon agreed. He put his arm around Benny's shoulders, feeling lucky. Not everyone had a little brother who never held a grudge. Now three more ducks hopped into the tub, their orange feet paddling a mile a minute. What a sight!

"Aren't they amazing, Mama?"

"To tell the truth, they look a little crowded. But they seem to enjoy the swimming place you made, Simon," Mama agreed. She turned back to the kitchen.

The first duck climbed out. Good. Simon remembered the pamphlet saying to be sure ducks can get out of their swimming water. Two more flopped in. Simon watched a bit longer and then went into the barn to change the ducks' chopped straw bedding.

As his last chore of the day, Simon carried two more pails of water to the tub, to replace what had splashed out as the ducks flopped in. Then he leaned on the fence. Some of the ducks had gone into the barn, but five were enjoying a swim. Their pale feathers glowed in the dusk, and their quiet quackings sounded to Simon like a chorus of "Thanks, boy, thanks, thanks, thanks."

Bed had never felt so good, and Simon was asleep seconds after he sprawled out beside his brother. The next thing he knew, Benny was tugging at him.

"Wake up, Simon!" Simon could hardly hear his brother, because of the incredibly loud noises coming through the bedroom window.

"It's the ducks!" Benny yelled. He was right, Simon realized, though these quackings sounded like a hundred ducks, not twelve.

Running out of their bedroom, the boys bumped into Papa in his nightshirt. "What in the world is that racket?" Papa growled.

"The ducks, Papa! I bet a fox came to kill my ducks!" yelled Simon, taking the stairs two at a time.

But there was no fox to be seen. Ducks surrounded the tub, quacking at the top of their lungs. What could they be quacking about? Simon peered into the tub. Oh, no! Where did the water go? In the bottom of the empty tub four ducks squawked. They stretched up, heads thrown back, bills pointing to the bright moon overhead, quacking indignantly, for all the world like little kids having a tantrum.

Papa started to laugh, stifling a chuckle at first, then whooping and wheezing, the tears running down his face. Simon could see Benny trying not to smile. He jumped in the tub and lifted the distressed ducklings out one by one. Gradually, the flock began to quiet down.

"What happened to the water, Simon?" Benny asked. Simon shrugged. The plug still sat in the drain hole, sealed off with putty, the way he had left it.

He shooed the ducks into the barn and closed the door. The last thing he wanted was ducks falling into the empty tub.

Rachel and Mama, with a fussing Sophie in her arms, stood on the back steps. "Your crazy ducks probably woke everyone in Melrose," grumbled Rachel.

"Simon," said Mama, as he passed her, "your ducks, I'm not sure they were a good idea. Your Papa needs his sleep, you know. We all do. We'll have to keep the ducks in the barn every night if this happens again. I hope that awful quacking hasn't waked up all our neighbors."

"I'm sorry about the noise, Mama," Simon murmured, as he trudged up the stairs. In bed, he tried to figure out what could have gone wrong with the tub, but fell asleep before he got very far.

First thing in the morning, a sleepy Simon stood in the duck yard, looking down at the tub. In a gap between tub and hole, he could see muddy, wet soil. He climbed into the tub and ran his fingers over the seams in the tin walls. Yes. Dang, double dang! He could feel a gap where two seams met. That's why someone had thrown out the tub! Perfectly good? Hah! He should have known that folks didn't throw out perfectly good things.

Dragging a couple of old boards out of the barn, Simon covered the tub so neither people nor ducks would fall in. He'd have to pull the thing out and somehow get it back to the dump, but he couldn't face that awful job right now.

When he came in for breakfast, Simon told the family his discovery. He ended, "The ducks must have been swimming as the water leaked out. Then they couldn't swim and they couldn't climb up the steep sides. That's when they began that awful squawking."

Papa, who had overslept and was taking a later streetcar into the city, stood up to leave. He gave Simon's shoulder a squeeze and said: "No great harm done, son, though it is a shame that you did all that work for nothing. You must admit that this will be a great story to tell the relatives!" He chuckled. Simon smiled weakly.

"Quack quack quack quack quack!" Rachel squawked, capturing perfectly the duck-yard clamor. Sophie, who always appreciated a good quack, joined in. And then everyone was laughing. Even Mama gasped for breath. Simon's face reddened, but he made himself smile.

The duck disturbance was a comical scene, he had to admit. Still, the fun of regaling Cousin Joe and the uncles with the story couldn't make up for all his wasted effort. He sighed. He knew his family would never let him forget his crack-brain idea of the duck's swimming pool.

15

The next day Simon listened for Mr. Avery's egg wagon. When he heard the familiar clip-clopping, he set down the pail of water he was carrying to the chickens and ran out to hail the egg man.

"You're not needing any of my eggs, are you, young Simon?" boomed Mr. Avery, pulling hard on the reins.

"No, sir, Mr. Avery, we have plenty of eggs. I have a question about ducks."

"Fire away then."

"I had a little tub and the ducks loved swimming there, but the tub leaked. Do you think it would be all right to let the ducks out to swim in the brook? I don't want to lose them downstream, carried away by the current. Maybe I could string chicken wire across the brook to keep them from straying."

"Well, now, seems to me ducks will pretty much stick together, close to their home territory. They know where their food comes from. About the fence, I don't know that you'd need it, but surely it wouldn't hurt. You shouldn't have a problem."

"Thanks, Mr. Avery" said Simon, thinking how he'd like nothing better than to have no problems with his ornery ducks! He patted the old horse's grizzled nose, then waved good-bye as he headed back to the chicken coop.

On Sunday, when the relatives arrived for another day in the country, they willingly followed Simon to the duck yard.

"You mean these strapping creatures are only six weeks old?" asked Uncle Herman, through clouds of cigar smoke. "Good grief, boy, you must be feeding them miracle food."

"And they'll be ready to sell in another month or so," said Simon proudly. I can't wait, he thought.

Benny broke in: "They'll each be seven pounds or more and the going price is fifteen cents a pound."

"And what will you young farmers do with all that money? Spend it all on comic books? …baseball gloves?"

"No, sir, Uncle Herman," Simon said. "We aim to buy a cow!"

"A cow? A cow? You really are getting to be farmers. What do you want with a cow?"

Simon explained the plan and how the money from the milk and the cheese and the butter would help out so that Papa didn't have to work so hard.

"Oh-ho, so you think we work your Papa too hard, is that it?" Uncle Herman frowned fiercely. But when he ruffled the boys' hair and beamed, they knew he was only joking.

"You're good boys, you know that? You know what means 'mensch?' It means a good person. We've got here a couple of menschen! Your Papa and Mama—they should be proud."

The aunts, who had been chatting with Mama, strolled over to see the ducks. "Do you have a place for them to swim?" asked Aunt Bella. So Rachel and Benny took turns telling about the fiasco of the swimming tub. Papa was right. Aunt Bella laughed. Uncle Herman and Cousin Joe howled. And Aunt Rose giggled until she hiccupped. Simon didn't even mind very much that the joke was on him.

Then Simon told about his plan to fence the brook. "Why don't we do that right now?" Cousin Joe asked. So Simon and Benny dragged the leftover chicken wire down to the brook while Joe took off his shoes and rolled up his Sunday trousers. They fastened the wire to a sapling on each side and weighted the bottom with heavy rocks. With Joe's help, the job went quickly.

Simon climbed up the bank and went to open wide the new gate he'd made in the duck yard. The boys and Joe watched the ducks flutter and strut their way to the brook and launch themselves into the flowing stream.

"Now you behave, you rascals," Joe said, "or I'll personally pluck your tail feathers the next time I come out!"

The last duck preening its feathers on the bank turned and fixed its beady eye on Joe. "Quaaaack!" it blared, making them all laugh.

The next morning, Simon picked two pails of ripe red tomatoes. Only a few had rotten spots: the ducks would like those. He could tell that Mama's first garden was a success, even though it was only August. Simon sat back on his heels to rest before carrying the pails in to Mama for canning.

He had grown to love the sounds of country living: the brook's burbling and the bees' humming in the tall hollyhocks by the door. What a change from the clatter and rumblings of his old Boston neighborhood! Even the birds sounded different. In the city, dusty sparrows squawked and squabbled over bits of food in the gutter, with a harsh "Cheep! Cheep! Cheep!" Today the cheerful song of a smaller sparrow perched at the top of a little maple tree kept him company. Its song made him smile: "Sweet-sweet-sweet… b-r-r-r!"

The next day he woke up to rain. When he came down to breakfast, Mama said, "Thanks for helping with the tomatoes yesterday, son. They wouldn't have survived this heavy rain. Folks think the rain will continue for days. They say it's the edge of an early hurricane, coming up the coast."

And Mama was right. Rain, rain, rain, day after day. Simon went to sleep hearing the steady drumbeat of rain on the tin roof over the kitchen, and woke up to the same sound.

Kept in the house all day, Sophie fretted. The chickens spent most of their time in the coop, and fussed at Simon when he came to collect the eggs. Only the ducks were enjoying the weather, trooping down to the brook that grew faster and wider each day.

On Thursday, Simon put on his oilskin rain gear and went to the feed store to buy corn for the chickens. He plodded home with the heavy sack on his shoulder, his galoshes squelching.

"Simon! Simon!" he heard through the noise of raindrops on his oilskin hat. He looked up and saw Benny coming toward him, slipping and sliding in the mud.

"The brook's flooded! Look at the ducks!"

The rain was too heavy for Simon to see clearly. He raced past Benny, dropping the sack. When he got close, he saw that the brook had overflowed its banks and the ducks swam happily over what had been dry land before.

The new pond had risen nearly to the top of the far bank beside the railroad tracks. Oh, no! Five or six ducks struggled up the bank. Two of them had already reached the top and waddled on down the tracks! Simon panicked. The four-fifteen train must be due any minute!

Simon tore off his oilskin and tossed it to Mama who rushed up breathing hard. "Where are you going, son?"

But Simon, running pell-mell, was already past her. He called back over his shoulder, "Mama. I have to bring back the ducks! I can make it. Just close your eyes for a minute!"

He heard his mama shout but in all the wind and rain couldn't hear what she was saying.

He reached the brook and took a running leap, but the stream was now wider and deeper than he thought. The current pulled him under and as he struggled, he had two thoughts: I don't know how to swim, and maybe these ducks *will* be the death of me. Fortunately, he came up coughing and set off half-wading, half-paddling, as he fought the powerful rush of the current. He went down again but struggled to his feet and climbed the bank. He heard the train, its brakes shrieking as it began to slow down for the long approach to the station.

Looking up the track he saw that he was too late. The train was here.

"NO!" he shouted into the wind and rain.

A huge blast of steam from under the engine drowned out his shout. The steam blew the ducks off the tracks, right back into the swollen brook! The engineer must have seen the ducks. As the train glided smoothly on toward Boston, Simon caught a quick glimpse of the engineer, waving. He yelled "Thank you!" into the wind and took a shaky breath.

Simon made his way back across the brook, more carefully this time. Benny had seen everything, but Mama hadn't looked after all. She said she couldn't bear to, so the boys took turns explaining how the ducks escaped disaster and got back to the brook.

"Simon Hirsh! You scamp! What am I going to do with you?"

"I'm sorry, Mama. I couldn't just let the train flatten our ducks."

Mama sighed and shook her head: "Look at the gray hairs you give me, son. But I *am* glad your troublesome ducks survived. It would be a shame to lose them after all your hard work."

The ducks waddled toward their pen. Their adventure must have made them hungry. Simon closed the gate firmly. No more outings for the ducks until the brook flowed safely within its banks.

Oh well, he thought, sitting next to the warm stove while his mother toweled off his dripping hair, at least this will show Rachel that Roaring Brook *is* a darn good name for that little stream. He sighed.

"Mama, I'm glad we're selling these troublesome creatures soon. I don't know if I can survive any more duck disasters."

"Myself also I cannot wait until your ducks are gone."

"Do you remember when Papa said I'd have duck dreams, Mama? It's been more like duck nightmares, wouldn't you say?"

16

One hot evening as Simon wandered down to the brook to cool off, he noticed a new sound: harsh buzzing noises, stopping and starting all around him. Were they frogs–or maybe insects? He'd never heard them in the city.

Out of the shadows he saw Patrick coming toward him.

"Hi, Patrick. Anything wrong?"

"Nope. Just wanted to tell you to wait for me Tuesday. That's the first day of school, you know. We can go together. I'll show you where our classroom is."

"Okay. Thanks." But Simon didn't feel thankful to be reminded how soon his summer freedom would end. Oh well, if he had to go, it would be better arriving with Patrick.

"Hey, Patrick, what's that buzzing noise? I never heard it before."

"Cicadas. They're sort of like grasshoppers. When they start up their racket, you know summer's almost over."

"Darn. I wish summer never ended. Don't you?"

"Yup. Sitting in a schoolroom's just about my least favorite thing." He started back toward the road. "Got to get home. See you Tuesday."

On Monday morning, after chores and breakfast, Simon saw Mama getting out her hair-cutting scissors and a towel. She pulled the tall kitchen stool over to the window. That meant just one thing: the back-to-school haircut for her boys.

"Ben! Help me muck out the duck pen," Simon muttered, but Mama grabbed him by the shirt as he headed for the door.

"The duck pen can wait, boys. I'm not sending ragamuffins off to this new school."

Benny went first, trying to read as Mama went to work. Then Simon perched on the stool while Mama snipped and combed, snipped and combed. You'd think she was giving a haircut to the President! "Ouch!" he yelped as the scissors nicked his neck.

"If you wouldn't fidget so much, Simon, that wouldn't happen, and I'd be done in half the time."

"Yes, Mama." Simon clenched his hands, forcing himself to sit still in spite of the snipped hair that tickled his nose.

By the time Mama finished, clumps of curls surrounded the stool and the breeze coming in the window felt cool on Simon's neck. "You look like a plucked chicken," Ben teased.

"Well, you look like a plucked duck, so there!"

"Off with you rascals! What you look like is respectable schoolboys, and you'll be cooler also." Mama shook the towel out the back door, then pecked Simon and Benny on the cheek as they slipped by her. Simon stripped off his shirt to shake out the tiny prickly hairs inside his collar that felt like needles.

At eight o'clock the next day, Patrick hollered from the road, "You coming, Simon?"

Simon grabbed his lunch box and gave Mama a kiss. "Benny! Hope you get a nice teacher!" he called over his shoulder.

The schoolyard was a jumble of strange kids, some squealing with pleasure as they spotted friends, others dragging along as if they were on their way to have a tooth pulled. Patrick was in the tooth-pulling group.

He hadn't said more than six words all the way to school, and here he might as well have been invisible.

He led Simon around the edge of the jostling crowd toward the front door. Just as they reached the entrance, a scowling heavyset boy loomed up and shoved Patrick into the wall. "Watch where you going, you big dumb Mick," he growled. Simon knew the Irish were looked down on. Still, hearing the hatred in that lummox's voice shook him up. But Patrick kept going, his long legs taking him up the stone stairway so fast that Simon was breathless when he reached the top.

"Here's our room," Patrick said, as if nothing had happened. "Guess we can sit anywhere." He headed for the back of the room.

Simon sank into a seat closer to the front. He'd never stay out of trouble if he sat in the back row. And he had to stay out of trouble, make a fresh start in this new school. Otherwise, Mama would never let him keep his chickens and ducks, let alone buy a cow.

He looked around. The fifth-grade classroom was just like the Boston schoolrooms he'd been cooped up in for years: a row of tall windows, a map pulled down behind the teacher's desk, an unsmiling George Washington staring out from his gilded frame. For a second, Simon felt as if the amazing changes of the last few months had been a dream.

But in the midst of all the boring sameness, something surprised him. At the chalk-board, a young man with a reddish-brown beard was talking to a student. His teacher was a man!

Simon was still trying to take in this surprising development as the classroom filled up. Then the teacher spoke: "Good morning, class. Most of you know that I'm Mr. Forrest. I'll be your teacher this year."

"We have two new pupils with us today," he went on. "Maria Santini and Simon Hirsh. Please welcome Maria and Simon and help them feel at home."

Simon made himself smile and look around at his classmates. Judging from her lowered head and blushes, the other new student had to be the dark-haired girl two rows over.

Mr. Forrest was rummaging in his desk when the same boy who had pushed Patrick hissed, "More damn greenhorns, I suppose."

"I'm NOT a greenhorn" slipped out before Simon could think. "I was born in this country and my parents are citizens! Besides, you shouldn't make fun of people who have just come to America."

"None of this rudeness and speaking out in my classroom," Mr. Forrest said, frowning. "Simon Hirsh, Martin Walters, do you hear me?"

"Yes, Mr. Forrest," grumbled Walters from the back.

"Yes, Mr. Forrest," Simon murmured. He felt like kicking himself. Why did he risk getting on the wrong side of his new teacher on the first day of school?

The rest of the morning Simon didn't raise his hand once. When the lunch hour came, the students who lived close to school headed home. "The rest of you are free to eat in the classroom or out on the schoolyard," Mr. Forrest said.

"Simon Hirsh," he said quietly. "Just to be sure we understand each other, I'd like to have a word with you before you leave for lunch."

Simon stood at the teacher's desk while Mr. Forrest erased the fractions lesson from the board.

"Now, Mr. Hirsh. What was so important that you had to start our day off by responding to the uncalled-for remark of another student?"

"I just wanted to say that it isn't right to tease greenhorns."

Mr. Forrest frowned. "Don't worry. I'll deal with Martin Walters and any other student who acts up. My advice to you is to ignore ignorant remarks. That's usually the best way to deal with them."

"Yes sir." Simon hung his head and made his way outside. He couldn't decide if he liked Mr. Forrest or not. He found a shady spot under an oak tree and opened his lunch box. He was cracking the shell of a hard-boiled egg when Patrick sat down next to him.

"You okay?" Patrick asked.

"Fine." Simon chomped on the egg.

Patrick's paper sack held only a thin sandwich. "What kind of sandwich is that?" Simon asked.

"Bread 'n bacon grease," Patrick mumbled, taking a big bite. Simon tried hard not to look disgusted, but it wasn't easy. Patrick's sandwich sure sounded unappetizing. And it wasn't much of a lunch for a big boy.

Patrick was looking at Simon's open lunch box with its thick tomato and cheese sandwich, fat carrot, and gleaming red apple. Mama had even tucked in a ginger cookie.

Wiping the crumbs of egg yoke from his lips, Simon offered his friend half a sandwich. "I'll trade," Patrick said, holding out the other half of his sandwich.

"Uh…no thanks. I can't eat bacon. It's not kosher."

Patrick's face showed that he didn't have the slightest idea of what kosher was, so Simon explained the basic Jewish rules about food:

nothing from a pig
no shellfish
only meat that had been slaughtered in a special way
no eating meat and milk in the same meal

"Sounds strange to me," Patrick said. Then he added, "Come to think of it, I guess we have one rule like that. Catholics can't eat meat during Lent."

Simon didn't know any more about Lent than Patrick did about kosher food.

"While you tell me what Lent is, have something, Pat. How about this apple?" Simon couldn't bring himself to give away the cookie.

"I'm fine," Patrick said and jumped up. He disappeared behind the school building. Simon ate the rest of the good lunch Mama packed, feeling bad for Patrick.

When he'd finished, he saw a group of boys with a ball. Patrick was just coming back around the corner of the school. "Come on, Pat. Let's get in this ball game."

Two boys were choosing up sides. "Fuzzy, get over here," said a tall kid with slicked-back hair. The other, the redhead who sat at the desk beside Simon, called, "I got Watson." He looked at the newcomers. "Jeez. Look who's here. Oh, well. You can have the kike, Jasper; I'll take the mick."

Patrick didn't say anything but ducked his head like he'd been punched. Though Simon was tempted to flatten the guy, he remembered

Mr. Forrest's advice. "Come on, Patrick," he said. "Dodge ball's a little kid's game anyway. Let's find something else to do."

When he looked to see if Patrick was following, he saw that a couple of boys who had been chosen for the dodge-ball game were coming as well.

"Want to see a wasp's nest?" said the skinnier of the two.

"Sure. Who are you?"

"I'm John. John Peters. Can't stand that ignoramus. This here's my cousin Raymond."

"Pleased to meet you," said Simon. The wasp's nest in a dead chestnut tree was interesting. And at least two kids had showed a little gumption.

Back in the classroom Mr. Forrest announced: "For fifteen minutes after lunch each day, I'll be reading to you." A stifled groan came from the back row. Mr. Forrest ignored it and started reading. He used different voices for all the characters. The beginning of the story was so gripping that Simon could hardly wait for the next episode. He wrote on the corner of his arithmetic paper the author's name: "Howard Pyle."

While he listened, he sized up his new teacher. Mr. Forrest was a small man, no taller than Simon's father, but he had impressive shoulders. And he certainly was in charge of this classroom. That was good, Simon had to admit. He didn't mind a strict teacher if she—or he–was fair.

As the students filed out, Simon heard Mr. Forrest say: "Martin Walters, I need to speak with you."

So when Mama asked later how the first day at his new school had gone, he could say, "All right, I guess." He escaped having to explain more when Rachel burst in, wanting to tell Mama every single thing about her day.

17

When Simon came in from school one frosty October day, Mama was waiting at the door. "Simon, Mr. Avery stopped by, wondering if you're ready to sell the ducks. Mr. Lee's been asking. His friend who owns the restaurant wants them next week."

"I sure am. How in the world, though, am I going to get twelve ornery ducks to Mr. Lee, Mama? I'll have to carry them two at a time. It'll take forever."

"Mr. Lee's friend–Mr. Fung, I think his name is—will send a wagon for them if he can have them now, Mr. Avery said. And he'll pay fifteen cents a pound, Simon. Imagine!"

A blast of cold air announced Benny's arrival. "Benny!" Simon said. "Guess what? Mr. Lee's restaurant friend wants the ducks next week and he'll send someone to get them. He'll pay fifteen cents a pound."

Benny stared at Simon. Without even stopping for the cinnamon cookies Mama had set out for them, he turned and trudged up the stairs.

Simon grabbed two cookies and followed Benny. He found his brother sitting on the bed, staring out the window.

"Hey, Ben, I brought you a cookie."

"No, thanks."

"What's the matter? Did one of those jerks bother you on the way home?"

Benny shook his head.

"Then what?"

Benny swiped at his eyes with his shirt sleeve. "I know we started raising ducks because you want to be a farmer and because we need to earn money for the cow," he said in a small voice.

"So?"

"Simon, the restaurant man is going to kill the ducks! People are going to eat them!"

Now it was Simon's turn to stare. "Of course they are, Benny. People will eat them just like we ate chicken last Friday night. What's wrong with that?"

"I don't know…," Benny's voice trailed off. His shoulders drooped. "We didn't raise that chicken," he muttered. Simon didn't have an answer to that.

Benny went on, "Doesn't it bother you to think about somebody killing our ducks? Remember how you worked so hard to make them a swimming pool?"

"Course I do. Thought my arms would fall off."

"And you nearly killed yourself trying to save them from being squashed by the train!"

Simon thought about what Benny was saying. "I guess it does bother me a little. But farmers have to be tough sometimes. More than anything, I want us to make this place a farm, and that means selling these ducks." He sat down beside his brother. "Tell you what, Benny. I need to sell these ducks, but from now on, we won't raise animals to be slaughtered."

"Really, Simon?"

"Really and truly. We'll build our flock of egg-laying chickens. We'll buy a cow and keep it for its milk. Rachel's cat will have her kittens. I didn't want another flock of ducks anyway. It was fun to see them swim and waddle around, but they were more trouble than they were worth. But Benny, you have to understand something," he went on. "Animals die, even if they're not raised to be someone's dinner."

"I know that." Benny's blotchy face broke into a weak smile. "Why do you think I'm going into the clothing business? Papa doesn't have to chase a suit around with a cleaver before he sells it, does he?"

"You noodle!" Simon called to his brother who was clattering down the steps, ready for his cookie.

On Saturday, a creaking old wagon pulled up to the door. "Moe's Packing and Hauling" was painted on the side in sturdy letters. And under that: "No job too small." A burly red-haired man jumped down as Simon ran out.

"You the duck farmer?" he asked.

"Yes sir," answered Simon. Even though he'd be glad to quit the duck-farming business, he liked the sound of that. "I'm Simon Hirsh."

"Hirsh, is it? I could be a landsman of your father's, my boy... from the same place in the old country. Where did your parents come from?"

Mama appeared, wiping her hands on a dishtowel. She and Mr. Moe began to talk and found out she and Papa and Mr. Moe had come to America from the same province in Russia. "Well, well... what do you know? I didn't expect to find a Jewish duck farmer," Mr. Moe said.

"And a Jewish wagon driver from a Chinese restaurant—who would think?" Mama said.

"Mr. Fung, he sticks to running his restaurant, you see. He hires me to do his hauling for him. If I'm not out traveling around peddling pots and pans, hair ribbons and scissors, I do hauling jobs."

Mr. Moe reached into the wagon and pulled out a scale. "If you'll bring me one of those ducks, Farmer Hirsh, we can get started."
Simon grabbed the nearest duck, making sure to tuck the strong neck and beak firmly under his arm. The peddler wrapped a chain and hook around the duck's feet, then let the bird drop. The bird quacked furiously while Mr. Moe read the weight on the scale's dial. Then he grabbed a crate from the wagon and popped the duck into it.

"Eight pounds, on the nose," he said. "Now let's crate up the rest of the flock. No need to weigh them all."

It took Simon most of an hour to round up and crate the other eleven ducks, but he knew better than to ask Benny to help with this particular job.

Mama and Mr. Moe had a good chat while Simon worked. He could hear them reminiscing about growing up in Russia, but soon they were sighing and shaking their heads about new anti-Jewish laws and the latest attacks by drunken mobs. Simon tried to ignore them. They were in America now. What was the use of talking about things that only made them sad?

After packing up the last duck, Mr. Moe pulled out a roll of bills and peeled off a ten and four ones. He then dug in his vest pocket and came up with four dimes. "Twelve eight-pound ducks at fifteen cents a pound. You've just earned yourself fourteen dollars and forty cents, young man."

"Only in America, eh, Missus Hirsh? It's a great country."

He hauled himself up on the wagon box and slapped the reins on the bony haunch of his old nag. "Shalom and mazel tov!" he called.

"Shalom," called Mama.

Simon stared at the bills in his hand. He held out the four one-dollar bills. "For the housekeeping jar, Mama."

"Now, Simon, that is what you earn with your hard work. The egg money comes in every week now to help with the housekeeping. Put that aside for your buy-a-cow fund. And you should keep some for spending money."

Simon shook his head. Then he remembered that Mama's birthday was next week. He and Rachel and Benny could buy Mama the warm shawl he had seen her fingering at the dry goods store.

Later, when Mama untied the package and saw the beautiful shawl in shades of soft blue, she stammered, "Oh, children! How did you know...?" She shook out the shawl and wrapped herself in it. "Pretty Mama," said Sophie, climbing into her lap.

Mama spread her arms and gathered under the soft folds Benny and Simon on one side and Rachel on the other. "You shouldn't have spent your hard-earned money, children," she murmured, "but it's the prettiest shawl I've ever seen."

18

When November came, the cheerful colors and the sunny crisp days of fall vanished. A cold spell set in. Simon finished his spelling test and looked out the window at the pine trees swaying in the wind, black against the gray sky.

He shivered. He and Benny would have another cold walk home by themselves because Patrick had missed school again. In fact, Patrick hadn't come all week, he realized. He must be sick.

As if he were reading Simon's mind, Mr. Forrest came over and said, "You live not far from Patrick Keegan's house, right? Would you take him this packet of work? I don't want him to fall too far behind."

So after school Simon didn't stop at home, although his face was stiff with cold and his feet and hands numb. "Tell Mama I'm going over to Patrick's, Benny. I won't stay long."

Before he reached Patrick's, a freezing rain started. Simon looked forward to a few minutes in a warm kitchen before heading back home. But when Patrick answered his knock, Simon stepped into a house that was not much warmer than the outdoors.

"Mr. Forrest asked me to bring you this schoolwork, Patrick," he said. "You've been missing so many days he's afraid you'll have a hard time catching up. Guess you've been sick."

"Yep. Had some kind of flu or something. Now the little ones got it." He gestured with his head toward the next room.

"Who's that, Pat?" a whiny voice asked. "Is that your friend Simon? Bring him here."

"He didn't come to see you kids, Mary Catherine."

"So what? I want to see him. If he doesn't come in here, I'll wake up Mama."

"You wanting him to get sick too? He's staying out here."

"Then you come."

Patrick shrugged at Simon. "My Ma's sick too. I better see to Mary Catherine. Ma needs her rest."

Simon peered into the tiny bedroom from the doorway. Four little kids were packed into one bed, under a blanket so worn you could nearly see through it.

One of the twins, who looked to be Sophie's age, whimpered weakly, over and over, "Mama, Mama, Mama."

A girl who was a little bigger looked feverish, thrashing around in the bed. That must be Maureen, the sister Patrick found a chair for at the dump.

Mary Catherine, who was probably six, reached up and pulled Patrick's head down. Simon heard her whisper, "Did he bring anything for us to eat, Patrick? I'm so hungry."

"Hush your face, for God's sake," Patrick growled. He came out and closed the door.

"Is your Pa sick too?" Simon blurted out.

"Naw. He's at work—works double shifts when he can get 'em." He opened the door. "Come on. You best be getting home before the storm gets any worse."

Plodding home, Simon couldn't stop shivering. Stepping into his mother's warm kitchen with the kerosene lamps glowing and chicken soup bubbling on the wood stove seemed like the end of a bad dream. He thought of Patrick's cold, hungry family and shuddered. After dinner, he'd tell his mother about it. She'd know how they could help.

"Where's Mama?" he asked Rachel, who stood at the stove, stirring the soup.

"In her bedroom. A letter from Russia. She'll be sad again. I said I'd finish getting dinner while she reads it." Simon held his tingling hands close to the stove and rubbed them. "Here, slice this loaf of bread, Simon, will you?" Rachel asked.

"Benny! Dinnertime!" she called, stooping to pick up Sophie. She set her in the high chair and began ladling out soup as Simon struggled with the big knife. Mary Catherine's pitiful question rang in his ears: "Did he bring us anything to eat?"

Mama appeared in the doorway, her eyes red and her cheeks wet.

Sophie looked up. "Mama no cry," she ordered.

Mama smiled. "This time, your Mama is crying for happy, little one." She dabbed at her eyes with her handkerchief and beamed at them all. Simon was on the verge of telling Mama about the cold and hunger and sickness at Patrick's shack, but he caught himself. If Mama was happy after reading the letter, he couldn't spoil that with his worries. They could wait.

Mama began: "Children, my news is so wonderful I need to share it with you all. My darling Rifka, my little sister, has saved enough for her ticket! She'll be coming across the ocean on a big ship to join us. At last, at last."

"Oh, Mama," Rachel said, dropping the ladle with a clatter and turning to hug her mother.

"Aunt Rifka," Simon murmured. He pictured the pretty young woman who gazed out of the faded photograph on Mama's dresser walking down a ship's gangplank.

Mama plopped down in a chair and lifted her apron over her face. After a moment, she lowered it and wiped her eyes. "Your Uncle Morris and I have been sending a bit of money when we could, but I thought it would be years before Rifka would have enough for a ticket. Oh, I can hardly wait to tell your Papa!"

Mama let the three older children stay up until Papa got home. "We will all rejoice together," she said.

When Papa came home and heard the news, he swept Mama into his arms. "She'll live with us, of course," he said, "at least for a while. Oh Eva, think of it! She'll know our children! And what a help she'll be to you!"

"I can hardly believe it," Mama said. She reached up and pinned back her hair, which Papa had knocked askew in the excitement.

"It seems like—what do they say?—a dream come true." Her face grew more serious. "Until Rifka is safely here, though, I worry. Her letter says things are getting worse every day. Food shortages are everywhere. Every day new rules. The police have forbidden Cousin Feyvel to take in boarders. And would you believe it, Ezra? Only the goyish hotel, the one run by Christians, is allowed to rent rooms. But they won't rent to Jews, of course. What a mad world it is!"

"I'm sorry, children," she broke off. "We will be happy for this good news and pray that dear Rifka's journey goes smoothly. Now off to bed with you."

Simon gave Mama a big hug. His news of the Keegan family could wait until another time.

That night, Simon bolted up from a bad dream, ready to run to Sophie's crib. He was awake now, but could still see and hear the dream Sophie, flushed with fever, calling over and over, "Mama! Mama! Mama!" He tiptoed down the cold hallway and stood outside Sophie's door, listening to her peaceful breathing. As he climbed back into his still-warm bed, he still couldn't get out of his mind the whimpering children in that cold shack.

19

The next day after school, Simon looked for a pencil to do his homework. Under a pile of old homework papers, he found the pamphlet on raising ducks that Mr. Avery had left last Fourth of July. Gosh, that seemed a long time ago. He didn't need it for ducks anymore, thank heaven, but on the back he noticed titles of other pamphlets. One was named "The Family Cow." Good, the pamphlet was free! Maybe this would be as helpful as the one on ducks had been. And he needed something to think about instead of the cold shack with its sick little kids.

Homework forgotten, he took a piece of notebook paper, and in his best penmanship, he asked for a copy of the cow pamphlet and addressed an envelope to the state Agricultural Extension Bureau, squeezing the letters to get the last word in.

Mama gave him a two-cent stamp, and he propped the important-looking envelope on his bureau. He'd put it in the mailbox in the morning.

The next morning Simon woke up early, hearing Mama and Papa talking in the kitchen. Their soft voices rose with the warm air through the square register in the bedroom floor. Mama sounded upset.

Simon eased himself out of bed so as not to wake Benny. Grabbing his sweater from the chair, he sat on the floor next to the open register.

"I hope she found an honest guide," Papa said. "A cousin of mine paid a fortune to a no-good wastrel who deserted them halfway to the border."

Fragments of Mama's softer voice drifted up. "….never forget how terrified I was when I made that night journey. …so dark….managed to avoid the checkpoints, but so many were sent back."

Simon crept back to bed. Mama's worries were worse than his Patrick worries, he had to admit. There was no need to get up yet, but he couldn't get back to sleep. The stories that he'd overheard aunts and uncles, neighbors and friends tell began creeping into his mind. Aunt Rose even had a cousin who landed in America and was sent back because she had a bad cough. Stop! he told himself. After all, look how many Jews made it—millions! Aunt Rifka would arrive safely. She had to, for Mama's sake.

All of this pushed the Keegans out of Simon's mind, until he saw Patrick slip into the classroom just as Mr. Forrest was handing back reports on the Battle of Bunker Hill. Simon slid his report into his book bag. Not only was there an "A" at the top, his first ever, but Mr. Forrest had scrawled, "Good work."

At lunchtime, Simon found Patrick alone in the back of the classroom. He put half an egg sandwich on Patrick's desk. Pat pushed it away but Simon wouldn't take it back. "Don't like egg salad," Simon lied. To change the subject, he asked, "Is your mother feeling better?"

"She's still poorly. Dizzy when she tries to get up. But she made me come." He wiped a bit of egg from his upper lip. "Ma doesn't want me missing too much school. She's set on my graduating eighth grade at least."

After school, Simon waited for Patrick. As he pulled on his warm hat and mittens, he noticed that his friend had only a collar to turn up against the cold and wind.

They walked in silence.

Finally, Patrick asked, "Your folks are immigrants like mine, right? How come you're not poor?"

Whew! That was a tough question. He didn't think his family was rich, but compared to the Keegans they were.

Patrick didn't wait for an answer. "My Pa got to America with only two dollars in his pocket. Took everything he had to pay for his ticket."

"My father says he had only enough for a week's room and board when he landed," Simon said. "But his brother and cousins had come before him. They started out selling clothes from a pushcart. After a few years, they saved enough to rent space for a store. They gave Papa a job. At first, Hirsh Brothers sold suits mostly to other immigrants."

"Huh! He was lucky then. None of the Irish had a pot to piss in when they got here. Even though the potato famine was sixty years ago, everybody's still poor as dirt." Simon had heard of the awful potato famine, when the only crop most Irishmen grew just rotted in the fields. Patrick's voice sounded bitter. "And when the Irish like my dad got to this wonderful 'land of opportunity,' no one would give them work."

Simon nodded. He had seen the signs: "No Irish Need Apply."

"My Pa's a smart man," Patrick went on. "He can fix anything. But the only job he could get is in this blasted rubber factory. The work's dangerous with vats of hot rubber and machines that go faster than a man can keep up. Every week or so, someone loses a finger, or worse." Patrick was raging now, kicking stones out of the road as if they were the cause of his family's misery.

"His pay is six dollars a week! Ha!" His voice cracked. "Can you believe that? Most of it goes for rent on the crummy shack!"

They were at Simon's house now. "Come in and get warm, Patrick." Patrick shook his head. "Got to get home."

"Wait a minute, Patrick. My mother's got so much cabbage, it's going to spoil. Just hold on while I grab a head or two."

He dashed in before Patrick could say no. "Mama, I'm home," he called. But Mama and Sophie weren't there. Oh, right. Marketing day. Well, Mama wouldn't mind. He knew feeding the poor was a mitzvah–a good deed. He raced down to the root cellar and grabbed a gunny sack, then stuffed in two heads of cabbage and a fistful of carrots.

"Thanks, Simon," said Patrick when Simon thrust the sack at him, "but don't think you have to do this. We'll be all right."

"I know."

"There is something you could do for me, though. I need someone to help me get some firewood. Meet me after supper tomorrow and lend a hand?"

Simon hesitated. After supper it would be dark. But Patrick was his friend and his family was cold and hungry. How could he say no?

He shrugged his shoulders and muttered, "Okay, I guess. But why does it have to be after supper? Where will you get firewood, Pat?"

"It's all stacked up in the town woodlot, next to the park. Been there for weeks. Nobody wants it, I guess. I don't have time to be chopping down trees."

"But Patrick..." Simon began. "You can't just...."

"I tell you, Simon, I'm taking this, but I need help hauling it."

"But what if someone..." His voice trailed off. Patrick was loping down the road, the sack over his shoulder.

20

No, you may not go to Patrick's after dinner to help him study for the test. Bring him here after school tomorrow and do it then." Mama went on chopping the hickory nuts the boys had found and shelled, but her voice was firm. "I won't have you out after dark on these roads, and snow is coming, they say."

Simon knew Patrick would be waiting for him. He thought of how cold that little shack had been. He turned and left the kitchen. Even if he told Mama how bad things were at the Keegan place, she wouldn't let him help Patrick move the wood. Not a chance.

That night, Simon waited until Benny was asleep, then scooped up his clothes and tiptoed down the stairs. In the cold, he fumbled with all his buttons and could hardly tie his bootlaces. The back door creaked horribly, but no one stopped him as he set out down the road.

Simon could hardly hear his own tapping on the door of the shack, but Patrick slipped out, quiet as a shadow. "For gosh sake, Simon, what took you so darn long?" he growled as they set out.

Simon didn't answer. A full moon made the going easier, but Simon was cold and miserable. He tried to keep from thinking about what they were going to do, but it was no use. They were going to steal the wood.

"Pat, I don't think this is a good idea. What if we get caught? We could be thrown in jail, you know."

"I told you. This wood's in the town woodlot. What does the town need wood for? They probably just cut up fallen trees to keep the woods neat. We'll be doing them a favor. It's not like stealing wood from a person."

Simon sighed. He knew Patrick was fooling himself, but maybe no one would miss the wood. Now he just wanted to get it over with.

"We need to stop at your place for the wheelbarrow," Patrick said.

"What? You didn't say anything about that!"

"Want to mess with that broken-down baby carriage instead? It would take us all night going back and forth to get enough wood for a week!" Simon sighed. He felt like he was up to his chin in quicksand and might as well give up. Who could reason with quicksand?

Pushing the squeaky wheelbarrow, Simon followed Patrick into the town wood-lot, next to the park where Simon had first met Patrick. The family picnic and three-legged race seemed to have happened to another boy in another life. Simon trudged into the dark trees, resigned now and just wanting it all to be over with.

Patrick shoved him and croaked "Get down!" Both boys dropped to their knees behind a row of shrubs. Simon slowly lifted his head and peered over the top, then shrank down again. The fatter of the town's two policemen was sauntering through the park, swinging a mean-looking nightstick. Motionless, the boys waited until Simon thought his blood had turned to ice. When the officer was out of sight and hearing, Patrick stood and crept into the woodlot with Simon at his heels. Once they got into the closely planted rows of pine trees, Simon could hardly see where he was going, but he followed the sound of Patrick's footsteps, straight to a pile of logs beside the path.

Loading the wheelbarrow seemed to take forever. Patrick said he'd watch for the policeman while Simon worked on the logs. Oh, right, Simon thought, so now I'm the thief, but he was too tired to protest. His gloved hands felt numb with cold. When there wasn't room for another log, he picked up the handles and started the load moving. Patrick joined him, then turned back and grabbed a small axe that someone had wedged in a nearby tree.

"I suppose nobody owns that either?" Simon spit out, straining with the heavy load, his muscles burning and his back already aching.

"I need it to split the wood. Don't you know you have to split logs before you burn them in a stove? I'll be done with it in a couple of days. I'll bring it back before anyone notices."

Simon shook his head and plodded on. Navigating the frozen ruts in the road took all his strength. Halfway home, Patrick seized the wheelbarrow and shouldered Simon out of the way.

When Simon's house came into view, Patrick growled, "I can handle it from here." Simon just nodded. Numb with cold, wearier than he'd ever been, and hardly able to lift one foot in front of the other, he trudged up the drive to his own kitchen. How warm and inviting the lamplight looked, shining in the window.

He stopped short. The lamp shouldn't be lit at this hour! Oh, no! Sure enough, Mama appeared at the door, wrapped in a quilt, her nighttime braid hanging over her shoulder. She looked angrier than Simon had ever seen her.

"There's that rogue Patrick!" she said, craning her neck to see around Simon. "I knew he'd be involved in this. Studying! Hah! What is that he's pushing?"

"I can explain, Mama."

"So explain." She folded her arms and glared. "I want to hear what's going on that makes you lie to your mother and disobey her."

Mama's face got even redder as she heard about taking the wood, but it softened just a little as Simon told about the frigid shack, the sick mother, the children whimpering with cold and hunger. "Patrick is trying so hard to take care of them, Mama. How could I say I wouldn't help him?"

"Simon, Simon. It is helping him to encourage him to steal? Why is it only now that you tell your Mama about all this?"

"I was going to tell you, Mama, and ask you what I should do. But then the news came about Aunt Rifka. I didn't want to upset you when you were so happy. Besides, I knew you'd say no, Mama."

"That's no reason, Simon. Foolishly you act, without thinking." She shook her head. "I thought you were learning better, son. This is something much more serious than your classroom misbehavior, you know. I won't wake your Papa now, but we will discuss this with him tomorrow night."

"Oh, Mama…" Simon felt tears coming.

"I knew that boy was a bad influence. I'm sorry for his family's troubles. Perhaps is a way we can help. But, Simon, you must use better judgment. I don't want you to play with him. Do you hear me?"

"Yes, Mama."

The next night, when bedtime came, Mama asked Simon to remain in the living-room. Rachel and Benny looked back as they climbed the stairs, questioning Simon silently. He dropped his head. They would know all about his disgrace before long.

"Papa, I'm sorry to tell you that Simon is in serious trouble," Mama began. Simon had to tell the whole story again. He didn't try to make excuses this time. He knew Mama was right. He should have come to his parents.

He thought he was prepared for any punishment. But Papa's first words hit him like a blow.

"You make me ashamed, Simon. What will our new neighbors think when this is known? No one in our family has ever been a thief! Some of our neighbors were taught that Jews are thieves and that the Irish are lazy no-good people. We need to show them by how we act that they are wrong. And then you and your friend Patrick do this!"

Papa sank into his chair, holding his head in his hands. The ticking of the mantel clock filled the room. At last, Papa looked up at Simon. "You and I will go to the town hall and tell someone. We'll find out what the wood is worth. You will pay for it from your savings for the cow. This is right. This is what we will do. Do you understand?"

"Yes, Papa," Simon whispered. He swallowed. The lump in his throat felt as big as a baseball.

"And you can forget about your farm. There will be no cow and you will sell the chickens. Once again you do a thing without thinking."

Simon was crying now. "I know it was wrong, Papa. But I did think." He gulped back his tears.

"I knew I might get in trouble, but that didn't seem as bad as Maureen and Mary Catherine whimpering all day and night because they were cold, and the twins feverish, and all of them hungry."

He dragged his sleeve across his wet face.

From the stairs came Benny's small voice: "Papa, Mama, Simon wasn't being bad."

Simon and his parents looked around. There on the stairs crouched Benny. Behind him sat Rachel.

Rachel blurted out, "We couldn't help hearing. Benny's right, you know." Simon stared at his big sister. "This time he made a mistake, but it wasn't because he didn't think first. That poor family! I think he was acting like a mensch."

Papa beckoned the eavesdroppers into the room, and sank into his chair. He looked like he might cry himself.

Simon could hardly breathe, waiting for Papa or Mama to speak. His feelings were all mixed up. This was the nicest thing Rachel had ever done for him, but it didn't change how ashamed he was.

Mama broke the silence. "What Rachel said is true. You have a good heart, my son, and the Talmud tells us that nothing is more important than that."

Simon's tears welled up.

Papa spoke up: "Your Mama and I know you wanted to help. That begins to explain how you could make such a bad mistake. But that doesn't change what we must do. You will pay for the wood. And tomorrow we will talk and find a better way to help that poor family. After that we'll think again about the chickens."

"And next time," Mama broke in, "you will ask our help before doing anything so…so…" She groped for the right word.

"So wrong," said Papa firmly.

"So wrong," Mama nodded.

"Yes, Mama. Yes, Papa. I understand."

"Now up to bed, all of you." Papa stood up and put his hand on Simon's head, the same gesture he used to bless each of his children every Sabbath eve. Simon felt the tightness in his throat ease a bit. His parents would help him make things right. And maybe, just maybe they would let him keep the chickens and save for a cow.

21

Mama met Simon after school the next day and marched him down Main Street to the town offices, so that Papa didn't have to miss work. Simon hung behind, dread weighing him down. But when they got to the town hall, with its big columns, it was Mama who hesitated. Simon led the way up the steps and into the building. He read the signs by each door, trying to figure out who would be in charge of woodlots.

He gave up finally, and asked a tall policeman who was sitting by the front door, reading a newspaper. "First door on the right, sonny," said the man, without looking up.

Simon could tell Mama was nervous, and he was, too. What if someone got this policeman to arrest him... *and* Patrick? What if they slapped him with a big fine for stealing town property, a fine so big that it was more than the cow fund, more than Mama and Papa could pay?

The man they needed sat behind a desk with a sign that said "Supervisor of Roads and Parks." He tapped a pencil and squinted under bushy red eyebrows as Simon explained what had happened.

Simon told the story without mentioning Patrick by name. Patrick had enough troubles without getting tangled with the law. And he'd hate to have his family's business all over town.

"We're sorry for what we did. We want to pay for the wood," Simon ended. "It was one wheelbarrow load. Can we do that?"

The man spun the pencil between his fingers and said nothing. At last he looked up. "I hope you young scamps have learned a lesson. If you hadn't come and confessed, you'd both be in hot water up to your eyeballs."

"Yes, sir." Simon held his breath.

"I could send you to reform school, you know. We got too many kids runnin' wild in this town. I've a mind to…"

Mama broke in. "Reform school? What is this reform school?"

"That's prison for young criminals, ma'am."

Mama's face went white. "Now just a minute, sir. My Simon is a good boy."

"Now, now, don't get all het up, ma'am. Just tryin' to scare a little sense into your 'good boy.'" He frowned and squinted at Simon.

"I'll go easy on you this time, kid. It'll cost you three dollars," the man said. "But if I hear you and your thieving friend are up to any more tricks, there'll be hell to pay. Understand?"

"Yessir," Simon muttered, hanging his head. "Thank you, sir." Digging in his pocket, he fished out three crisp dollar bills and handed them over with a small sigh. That cow seemed farther away than ever. If his parents would even let him have a cow.

Simon held out his hand and the man shook it. Mama thanked him and they started for the door.

"Just a minute there," the man called.

Simon's heart sank. What now?

"You can tell your friend that if his folks come down here and sign up, they can get coal to see them through the winter. In Melrose we take pride in looking out for folks who are hard up, especially when they've got kids."

Whew! Simon turned. "I'll tell them, sir. Thank you."

As he came out into the fresh air, Simon felt as if a gray cloud had blown away.

"You're a good boy, Simon," Mama said, as they came down the steps.

"Thank you, Mama. But there's one more thing. I have to get the axe and return it. And I need to tell Patrick about the coal."

Mama sighed. "I understand. Do that, son, and when you get home, I'll make up a sack of potatoes, apples, and bread for you to take to Patrick's tomorrow. I know Patrick and his parents are proud, but they'll accept for the children's sake."

Simon took a deep breath. "Mama, Patrick isn't bad. He doesn't mind working hard and he's a good brother. I think I'm the only friend he's got. We've both learned our lesson, truly, Mama. Please let me go on being his friend."

Mama sighed. "All right for now....but only if you promise to behave. No more crazy ideas."

"Yes, Mama."

Simon trudged toward the weather-beaten gray shack. Patrick was in back of the house, stacking a neat pile of split wood against a tree. "Patrick, I have to tell you something. Our stunt the other night got me in real trouble." Patrick went on stacking the wood and Simon plunged ahead, describing the scene at the town hall. Patrick said nothing but his neck got redder and redder.

When Simon finished, Patrick whirled around and spit out: "I can't believe you went and ratted on us! What did you want to do that for, you... you... traitor! I feel like knocking your block off!" Patrick was nose to nose with Simon but pulled back and wheeled away, pacing furiously back and forth.

"Do you think it was my idea, Pat?" Simon snapped. "I got dragged down there! My father said it was the right thing to do and when he feels that way, there's no stopping him."

"Humph!"

Simon glimpsed Mary Catherine's pale, pinched face squinting through a dirty windowpane. "I didn't rat on you, Patrick. Honest. Nobody knows who was with me that night."

"No, but if they find out, I'll get all the blame 'cause you got scared and fessed up like a goody-goody."

"Patrick, the man said we were square, once I paid the three dollars. He isn't going to come after you. Besides, he says your folks can get free coal from the town to tide you over this winter."

"You think my Pa would take charity? He'd sooner die."

"So taking charity is worse than stealing? And what about the little kids? What are they supposed…"

Patrick lunged forward and knocked Simon to the frozen ground, then punched hard. Simon fought back and landed a good uppercut to Patrick's chin. Through clenched teeth Patrick growled, "You shut up about my family. Keep your lousy Jew nose out of our business or I'll strangle you."

Simon was stunned, more by the words than the blows. He just lay there. After a moment, Patrick rolled away and got up, his back to Simon.

"I never should have trusted you. My uncle told me, and Father Haggerty too. 'You can't trust kikes; they're dirty, greedy, money-grubbing bastards,' they tol' me. 'They were Christ-killers, you know.' "

Simon felt sick. Could this be America? Patrick sounded like the louts who attacked Jewish villages—even old men and babies—back in Russia.

He wiped his nose on his sleeve and saw blood. Without saying a word, he picked up the sack of food his mother had sent, dumped it all on the ground, and started for home, grabbing the axe from the wood pile as he passed.

He wrapped the axe in the sack and, his mind numb, headed for the town woodlot. After checking to be sure no one was looking, he sank the axe into a tree close to where Patrick had found it. With that done, the numbness thawed and feeling rushed back. A few tears trickled down his stiff cheeks. He swiped at them, swallowed hard, and headed home.

22

When Simon finally reached home, he went straight to his room and flopped facedown on his bed. Footsteps came pounding up the stairs.

"Simon!" Benny burst in. "We've been waiting supper for you! You still have your coat on…and your overshoes! What happened? Are you sick?"

Simon sat up and looked at his younger brother. He could never tell Benny what happened. Or Mama either. He could never repeat those poisonous words, not in a million years.

"What happened to your nose, Simon? Did you get in a fight?'

"Didn't you ever have a nosebleed, Benny, for gosh sakes? I'm just tired and I'm not hungry. Leave me alone, okay?—and tell Mama I have homework to do."

"But Simon…" Benny broke off, and then Simon heard him start down the stairs.

No sooner had the clatter of Benny's feet faded than Simon heard more footsteps on the stairs. Was Mama sending Rachel to bring him down? He looked up to see Mama herself.

"I'm guessing that Patrick didn't take the news very well. Is that right, son?" Simon nodded.

"Well, I'm not surprised. But he'll get over it. Come get your supper. I made kugel with raisins, just the way you like it."

Simon sighed and followed his mother down to the kitchen. He ate a bit of kugel. Rachel chattered away about a play her class would put on in the spring, and Benny kept making Sophie squeal by stealing her raisins, so no one seemed to notice that Simon wasn't himself.

For days, Simon couldn't get the fight and the words out of his mind. He wished Mama would quit trying to get him to talk about what was wrong. One morning just before he left for school, Mama said: "Simon, you haven't been the same since our trip to the town hall. Is it the money you had to pay? Soon it will be Hanukkah, you know, and you will have some Hanukkah gelt to build up your savings."

"I know, Mama. It isn't the money."

"Well, what then? Patrick is not speaking to you? For that, I wouldn't worry. As I said, that won't last. And if it does, he wasn't a real friend."

"Yes, Mama," muttered Simon. He felt like snapping, "Just leave me alone!!" Of course, he couldn't yell at Mama, so he walked out of the room instead.

Once when Simon was doing his homework, he noticed Mama watching him. She gave her head a little shake before she turned back to ironing Papa's shirt. And soon, Papa seemed to be watching him too.

Late one night, when Benny was fast asleep, Simon heard a soft knock on the door and Papa let himself in. He sat on the bed and rubbed Simon's back. "Simon, you know your mama and I worry about you. No more mischief-making, no more teasing Rachel, no more making big farm plans. Is this my Simon?"

Simon turned over and made himself smile.

"Son, I think I can guess what's been on your mind. But I think that if you can't repair your friendship with Patrick, you can make new friends. That would surely help."

"But Papa, I do have other friends now. John and Raymond and I eat lunch together every day." Simon wished that he *could* tell Papa about the fight and the terrible things Simon said about Jews, but it made him feel sick just to think of it. And he didn't want Papa to get involved. Who knows where that might lead?

Papa took Simon's hand. "Perhaps you're worrying about whether we'll make you sell the chickens and give up the idea of getting a cow. Yes?"

Simon shrugged. He did worry about this but hadn't wanted to ask. Papa went on, "Here's what your Mama and I have decided. You know now that getting involved in the stealing was wrong. And Mama told me how proud she was when you confessed what you boys had done. That was wise. If you hadn't straightened it out with the town and paid for the wood, and you boys were found out, the consequences would have been worse for Patrick and his family than for us—because Patrick was the ringleader and because his family is so poor. His father might have lost his job."

Now Simon felt worse than ever. Did Papa think this would cheer him up?

Papa went on. "Another thing, son. I think your decision to tell Patrick about the trip to the Town Hall was brave. And returning the axe was also brave. Your Mama and I have decided there's no need to sell the chickens. And if you can find a way to buy a cow, we'll help you make that a success too."

"Thank you, Papa," Simon said with a real smile and a hug. Papa squeezed his shoulder and stood up. "Now I'm not saying you should start getting into mischief and teasing your sister, you know. Your mother and I are getting used to the quiet around here."

Before Simon fell asleep, he decided that he wouldn't even try to make up with Patrick. Suddenly he felt relieved. Being friendly with Patrick had never been easy.

Patrick came into the classroom the next morning, late as usual. When he passed down Simon's row, Simon ducked his head and rummaged around in his desk.

That day he invited John and Raymond to come over and see the chickens. The boys helped collect the eggs, after Simon told them how to do it without stirring up the hens too much. On Monday they all played marbles after school at Raymond's house. Doing things with his new friends did cheer up Simon, as Papa said it would.

But the next week, Simon couldn't help noticing that Patrick missed school every day. What was going on in the cold little shack? Was Patrick sick again? And how about the little ones? The weather had gotten colder. They couldn't have frozen to death, could they?

"Hey, Simon!" Halfway home on Friday, Simon turned to see Rachel, winding her long scarf around her neck and hurrying to catch up with him.

"Where are your girlfriends?" he asked. Rachel was rarely seen without her group of "best friends."

"Elizabeth had to stop at the Five and Dime to buy thread for her mother and the others went with her. I figured I'd better get home to watch Sophie so Mama can get on with Shabbat preparations."

They fell into step together. "Aren't you excited about Aunt Rifka's coming, Simon? I've been thinking she could move in with me. There's room for another bed. It would be like having a big sister!"

Simon had barely given a thought to Aunt Rifka's arrival since the day Mama got the letter. Rachel's offer impressed him. His sister loved her cozy front bedroom. She especially loved having it to herself, he knew.

He was even more impressed when Rachel went on to say, "...but then I thought, she doesn't know us yet. She'd probably rather have a room to herself. So it would be better if I moved in with Sophie."

"Golly, Rachel. Are you sure?"

"Well, I just want our new aunt to be happy here. But I think she will be. Melrose is such a pretty town and people are so friendly here."

"Don't be so sure of that." Simon scowled and kicked a chunk of ice down the road. "Remember, Aunt Rifka doesn't speak much English. She'll just be a 'greenhorn' to most people. I hope she doesn't think she's coming to some kind of paradise. People hate Jews here, too, you know."

Rachel stopped in her tracks. "Simon Hirsh! What are you saying? What makes you think that?"

Simon kept walking. "Oh, never mind. Come on. We'd better get home to help Mama."

Rachel followed, shaking her head. "Sometimes I can't figure you out, Simon. I'd just been thinking you're not as moody these days, and here you go again."

They trudged along in silence, except when their overshoes crunched the icy patches. As they turned the corner to home, Rachel said, "Oh, I almost forgot... Patrick's sister Kathleen ran up to me in the hall today. She told me to tell you her father says thank you. Something about getting free coal. He didn't know how you found out about it, but he went down to the town hall and signed up. Kathleen said it would be a big help to their family this winter. Did Patrick say anything to you about it?"

Simon shook his head and slowed his footsteps as Rachel hurried into the house. So Patrick had been wrong about his father's pride. And he couldn't even apologize to Simon for what he'd said? Well, good riddance to that so-called friend.

At least the shack and all the little Keegans are warmer now. That's one less thing to worry about, Simon thought—not that it changes for one minute how I feel about my former friend Patrick.

From that day on, Simon and Patrick ignored each other. After a week, Raymond asked what had happened, but Simon just shrugged. Nothing more was said about it. Since Patrick had been a loner to begin with, Simon figured no one thought it was strange that the two of them were not doing things together.

23

Simon had completely given up hope of receiving the cow pamphlet when one cold December day he found in the mailbox a thick envelope addressed to Mr. Simon Hirsh. He raced into the house. This had to be "The Family Cow." With fumbling fingers he tore it open. Yes! He raced upstairs, clutching the pamphlet that would tell him all he needed to know about owning a cow. With the money from the sale of the ducks and the gelt he and Benny would get for Hanukkah next week, it shouldn't be long before they had all the money they needed to make the cow dream come true.

But Simon's excitement leaked away as he read the pamphlet. It seemed that buying a cow was only the beginning. Under "Supplies" he read: "3-legged stool, grain scoop, curry comb, udder cream, buckets." The list went on: "Churn, skimmer, strainer, paddle"—those were for making butter—then more things to make cheese. On another page: "At least 60 bales of hay in winter."

He read on: "A Jersey cow will yield two to three gallons of milk a day, at least six hundred gallons a year, plus a calf." That was more encouraging, but still, the amount of money he and Benny were saving up to buy a cow wasn't nearly enough to get started. In addition, they would need all these things to care for the cow and to turn the milk into butter and cheese. Simon flopped on the bed and buried his face in his pillow.

He heard Benny come in and dump his schoolbooks on the bed. "What's wrong, Simon?"

"Read this, Ben. We need a lot more money in the cow fund than we figured."

Benny studied the pamphlet. "You're right. This isn't good. Just look at all the equipment we'll need."

"And we'll have to buy a lot of hay. We don't have a hayfield."

Benny kept reading, as Simon got up and paced around the room. When Benny had read the whole pamphlet, he sat up. "Simon, maybe we could find second-hand stuff that wouldn't cost much. And selling the milk would help pay for the hay."

"But Benny, the biggest problem is that neither of us knows how to milk, how to churn, how to make butter and cheese. Making and selling butter and cheese, this says, are how you make money in dairy farming. That means the biggest problem is we'd have to hire someone to work for us who knew about dairy farming."

"And that would take real money," he ended, his shoulders sagging. Benny stared at Simon and after a few minutes, slowly nodded. "You're right. I should have thought of that."

A few days later, everyone was getting ready for the trip to Boston to join the family Hanukkah celebration. "Simon, you look so gloomy," said Rachel. "Aren't you excited about the party? It's always so much fun, and remember the Hanukkah gelt. I thought you said you boys might have enough money now to buy your cow when spring comes."

Simon shrugged. "I guess." He didn't feel like telling Rachel how wrong he and Benny had been.

The streetcar rattled along through glittering snowdrifts as they traveled back to Boston to Uncle Morris's and Aunt Rose's place. Simon's breath rose in frosty clouds. He pulled his head deeper into the wooly scarf wrapped around his neck and edged closer to his brother for warmth.

At their stop, Papa hurried them off. The red and yellow streetcar started up again, rattling and squealing on the tracks.

The uncles and aunts and cousins crowded into the hallway to greet the family. Papa handed Uncle Morris four quart jars of Mama's good applesauce, wrapped in layers of newspaper. "Careful there, Morris. This delicious treat came from our own apple trees."

Both Mama's and Papa's side of the family were there. When Simon spied Cousin Joe, he pushed through the crowd. "Hey, Joe," he said, as Joe grabbed him around the neck in a fake hammerlock.

Rachel was swept away by the older girl cousins and Aunt Bella cuddled Sophie. The aunts and Mama headed for the kitchen, chattering and laughing.

Simon and Benny joined the men in the parlor, who were talking of how good business was. Simon knew the delicious smell from the kitchen meant the women were frying a mountain of potato pancakes or *latkes* that would be served with the applesauce.

He overheard Papa saying, "A cold early winter is a gift when you are in the business of making the best overcoats in Boston. Our store is full of people looking for warm coats and suits." Papa chuckled: "Old Mr. Harper at the grocery store yesterday swore that this is the 'wust winta in fohty yee-ahs.' " The uncles laughed hearing Papa speak in that strange New England accent.

Soon the talk turned to boring stuff about the old country. "Let's start the dreidel game," Simon said. Rachel found the little four-sided top that Uncle Morris had set out on the lamp table. The children sat on the floor in the corner. Cousin Joe, who considered himself too old now to be a player, counted out hickory nuts to bet with —the same number to each child. Simon had been the winner last year. But when he heard the grown-ups talking about the hardships Aunt Rifka faced in her voyage, he lost his concentration and dropped out..

Uncle Morris said, "No doubt she'll travel in the cheap steerage section below deck, and be seasick, like we were. Remember how bad the stench of vomit was?"

Papa broke in: "…and we couldn't eat the awful food they serve—not only because it wasn't kosher but because it was vile-smelling. We barely had strength to wobble down the gangplank, remember?"

Simon had heard this many times and didn't want the grown-ups to spoil the Hanukkah celebration. "Papa, die kinder!" he said sternly, giving a nod toward Sophie, who was nearby rocking her doll.

Uncle Herman raised his eyebrows. "Eh? So we understand Yiddish now, do we, young man? No more secrets in this family, I suppose." He threw his head back and laughed, but the men changed the subject to the weather, and Simon went back to the game. Rachel was about to win.

After the menorah candles were lit and the blessings said, everyone feasted on delicious latkes, sour cream, applesauce, and rye bread. Then it was time for the children to receive their Hanukkah gelt. Simon and Benny's mouths dropped open—Rachel's too. It was twice as much as the uncles had given them last year. Seeing their astonished faces, Uncle Herman said, "Didn't we say this is the best year ever for the business? You boys will have your cow in no time."

"Thank you," Benny and Rachel said, but Simon couldn't speak as he stared at the coins, more money than he had ever seen at one time. He looked up. "This is wonderful. Thank you, everyone." He tried to sound happy. While he was thinking of a polite way to tell Uncle Herman that it would still be a long time before they could save enough for the cow and all the other expenses, quiet Uncle Morris spoke up.

"Now I have a surprise," he said. "more news." Everyone hushed. From the smile on Uncle Morris's face, Simon told himself it couldn't be bad news. Uncle Morris drew from his vest pocket an envelope with the strange stamps that meant it came from the old country. "This letter came just yesterday."

He began translating haltingly from Yiddish to English. Aunt Rifka was learning English, Simon knew, but used Yiddish for her letters. "Dear Morris and Rose," the letter began. "Please share this letter with all the family. I have been saving wonderful news until the plans for my voyage were firm. If all goes well, I will be sailing from Hamburg in early March and will arrive in Boston three weeks later."

"Hurrah," shouted Rachel and Benny. "Our new aunt is coming!"

Uncle Morris cleared his throat and went on reading. "Sister Eva wrote about my nephew Simon's longing for a cow and how hard he is working and saving. Also that little Benny is helping him. 'What do Ezra and I know about milking and dairying?' my sister Eva laments. Well, can you believe this? It is working for a farmer that I was able to earn enough to pay for my passage. He has three cows, and I've been helping with the milking and the churning and the cheese-making!

"I'll be able to teach you everything I know and also help you with the work. Now I feel much better about accepting Eva's kind..." Uncle Morris groped for the right word in English.

"Invitation?" suggested Rachel.

"Invitation," continued Uncle Morris, "... to live with Eva and Ezra and the children in Melrose."

Everyone turned to look at Simon and Benny, who were speechless. Cousin Joe was the first to speak. "Woo-ee! Now all you need is a cow, boys, right?"

Papa chimed in, "With the expert help your Aunt Rifka offers with the dairy chores, we certainly do need a cow. How much in the cow fund, Simon?"

"With tonight's Hanukkah gelt, we have about forty dollars, probably enough to buy the cow. But we learned we'll need equipment too—and lots of hay. With Aunt Rifka teaching us how to take care of a cow and helping with the dairy chores, we're getting close to having enough money, but we don't have quite enough yet—maybe next year."

The uncles put their heads together and talked in low voices. Then Uncle Herman announced that with business so good, the families can contribute twelve dollars more. "We calculate that might be enough to get you started, boys."

"Yippee," Benny crowed, but Simon tugged on Benny's shirt and whispered in his ear.

"You're right, Simon," he murmured.

Turning back to the uncles, Simon said softly, "That's too much. Every winter won't be so cold before the holidays, you know." Benny nodded sadly.

"Do you think we're doing something foolish, boys?" Uncle Herman bellowed. "This is a business deal. We'll be your investors. When your cow begins to give you milk and cream and your Aunt Rifka shows you and your mother how to turn it into butter and cheese to sell, you can begin repaying our investment."

Simon and Benny smiled shakily. Simon croaked, "Thank you, Uncle Morris and Uncle Herman. Thank you, Papa!" First Simon, then Benny, gave Papa a hug, but the uncles solemnly shook their hands. "Just like real business partners," Benny whispered to Simon with a grin.

Simon's worries melted away. Imagine his Aunt Rifka helping him learn to be a good dairy farmer! Mama isn't the only one who is pinching herself with the day's good news, he thought.

Part Two

24

Three months later Simon stood on the pier and stared at the building that loomed over the waiting crowd. He had never seen such a huge building. Over the door a sign said: New Immigrant Landing Station. The immense ship behind him had docked at the pier before dawn, Papa said. Hundreds of families had come to meet the passengers, but not a passenger was to be seen. Papa said they all had been herded into this huge building. "But why aren't they coming out, Papa?" Simon asked.

"The doctors need to look them over for signs of disease, and officials need to check their papers." Mama sighed. She hadn't smiled since they left home. "Now don't worry, dear," Papa said, stroking her arm. "We know Rifka is healthy, and her immigration papers are in order. I'm sure she won't be sent back."

Simon squeezed Mama's hand. The little sister she had to leave behind when she came to America had grown up and traveled to America on this very ship! Mama would be broken-hearted if they sent Rifka back to the old country, with all its dangers. But Simon, like Papa, felt sure their aunt would soon be with them. It was hard to worry with the sun dancing on the water, the flags on the building snapping in the brisk

March wind, and a whole day off from school. He had been the only one allowed to come with Mama and Papa. His job was to help Papa with Rifka's baggage. Unfortunately, Uncle Morris hadn't been able to come, even though he was Aunt Rifka's brother. Mama said he had a bad cough and didn't want to pass it on to anyone, especially not to his sister who was probably all worn out from the journey.

The minutes of waiting for Aunt Rifka stretched into an hour, then two. A few people trickled out of the building with steamer trunks and carpet-bags, but Papa said those looked like rich people. Poor immigrants had to wait—and wait.

The wind was cold and though he was wearing his heavy coat and his wooly winter cap with earflaps, Simon couldn't get warm. Not even blowing on his hands and stamping his feet worked.

Simon's excitement ebbed along with the tide. The new immigrants from the ship didn't come and *didn't* come.

Mama opened her satchel and brought out hard-boiled eggs and apples, but there was no way to make hot tea.

After another two hours, Papa said, "I'm afraid I need to get back to the store." He kissed Mama, waved to Simon, and headed for the streetcar that would take him to downtown Boston.

Now Simon really started to worry. The walk to the streetcar stop was long, he knew. Without Papa, how could they manage all of Aunt Rifka's baggage? Simon and Mama huddled together, trying to keep warm.

All of a sudden, Simon caught sight of Cousin Joe pushing through the crowd and his worries blew away in the wind. "How did you get off from work, Joe?" he called, running to meet him. He had never been gladder to see his favorite cousin.

"Well, when your papa got back to the store, he and my papa decided I could take the rest of the afternoon off to help with your Aunt Rifka's baggage. Not only that, I'm to go home with you on the trolley to Melrose."

But Joe was no better at waiting than Simon. After pacing back and forth a few times, he said, "Simon, my boy, come with me. Aunt Eva, I'll keep an eye on this rascal. A little exercise will do him good."

As Joe headed toward the building with long strides, Simon had to run to keep up with him. When they plunged into the crowd of impatient people, Simon grabbed Joe's hand. They walked past several entrances into the building. Unfriendly-looking men in uniforms stood at each door. Their faces reminded Simon of Miss Kane, his crabby fifth-grade teacher who had scowled at the immigrant children as if they were worthless. He was surprised when Joe dragged him up to one of the guards.

"Hello, there, Mr. Standish," Joe said. "How is the overcoat working out?"

The guard smiled. "Warmest one I ever had. And what brings you and this young sprout here, Mr. Hirsh?"

"We're here to meet the boy's aunt. I hear one of the officials is giving her trouble, probably because she has no one to watch out for her. Might we go in to help with her baggage?" Simon saw Joe take out a dollar bill and press it into the man's hand. The bill disappeared smoothly into a pocket and the guard stepped aside.

"Come in someday and see our line of spring suits, Mr. Standish," Joe said as they went in. "The fabric is smooth as silk and wears like iron."

A minute later Simon whispered: "How did you know someone was being mean to Aunt Rifka?"

Joe shrugged. "I *don't* know, but it's probably true. Come on, let's find your aunt."

Simon looked around the vast space. Babies wailed. Women scolded, trying to keep older children from wandering off. An old woman wrapped in shawls sat on a tattered bundle, staring into space. A few people, men as well as women, wept. One tearful man rocked himself back and forth as he lamented, "I knew when our Miriam's eyes began to ooze, she wouldn't be allowed to stay."

"Hush, hush," his wife murmured, "A few days, they said they would keep her and give medicine for the eyes."

A porter piled baggage on a hand-cart and wheeled it toward the door, with a big family trailing behind. Another porter came in and people rushed over, begging for help with their belongings.

Even Joe looked bewildered. He clapped his hand to his forehead. "What a dummkopf I am! How will I find your aunt? I don't really know what she looks like!"

"I'll recognize her, Joe. I've seen her picture a million times. She looks like Mama, only younger." But as Simon peered into one woman's face after another—calm or weeping, old or young, ugly or pretty—he wasn't sure he *would* recognize Aunt Rifka. But he couldn't give up. He wanted so much to take his new aunt away from this noisy crowd of desperate people and deliver her to Mama.

Just then he felt someone pulling on his sleeve. He whirled around and saw smiling at him the woman he knew from the portrait on Mama's bureau.

She was pale and rumpled but as beautiful as he knew she would be. Then his aunt drew him to her, "Shee-*mon*, Shee-*mon,*" she murmured, pronouncing his name as people from the old country did.

"But Auntie Rifka, how did you recognize *me*?"

"Your mama, may she be well, send me a picture of you and your brother and sisters. Every day I look at it, yes?"

Only then did Simon notice Joe, holding his hat over his heart, bowing a little toward Aunt Rifka. "Can't you introduce me to your pretty aunt, Cousin Simon?"

"Auntie Rifka, this is my cousin Joseph. He and his father, Uncle Herman, work with my Papa at the clothing store. And Joe, you must know that this is my Aunt Rifka."

"I do indeed. She's your mama's dear sister, the one we've all been waiting for."

With that Joe leaned down and hoisted Rifka's heavy trunk to his shoulder, then grabbed up her enormous bundle. Simon picked up two scuffed suitcases and trailed behind. None of the scowling guards stopped them.

Seeing Mama embrace her sister, with tears of joy running down her cheeks, all the troubles of the day melted away for Simon.

When they all reached the trolley, Simon fell into the seat beside Joe, behind Mama and Aunt Rifka. Never had he been so glad to sit down.

Mama and her sister chattered away, back and forth, shifting from English to Yiddish after a few minutes. Then his aunt's head drooped on Mama's shoulder and she seemed to sleep all the way to Melrose.

When the streetcar stopped, Joe and Simon grabbed Aunt Rifka's luggage and carried it home to a delicious tsimmes dinner that Rachel had warmed up for them. After dinner, Joe got up. "I'm off to catch the last streetcar," he said stretching his long frame.

"Joe," said Mama, "how can we thank you enough for all your help? I think we'd still be sitting on the luggage at the dock if you hadn't come."

Rifka said, smiling, "I also think, how can we move all this heavy baggages if Yosef is not here?"

Rachel beamed and gave Simon a look. He knew it meant: Isn't this romantic? He shook his head. Girls.

25

Aunt Rifka didn't appear at the breakfast table and she was still in bed when the children had to leave for school. To Simon, the day seemed endless. Mr. Forrest's explanation of the Spanish-American war dragged on and on, but finally the dismissal bell rang. Simon ran all the way home with Benny at his heels and Rachel not far behind. The cinnamon aroma of Mama's special apple cake greeted them. Even better, a rested-looking Aunt Rifka came to the door with an embrace for each child. At the table she looked around and said: "So children, tell me about your school."

Rachel plunged in, chattering away about her favorite teacher, while Mama served big slices of the warm cake. When Rachel stopped for breath, Simon broke in. He didn't tell Aunt Rifka about boring old school, he wanted to talk about farming. He had so many questions. "Aunt Rifka, tell us about your work at the dairy, back in the old country. Was it a big farm? How long did you work there? Did it take you long to learn to milk?"

"Well, nephew, in our village we had small farm. From a little girl, I go to the farm to watch whenever my Mama she have no work for me at home. The farmer, he tease me that the horse maybe nip me or the chickens scratch me, but they never did. I think the creatures knew how I love them. And I hear that you boys love animals, yes?"

"That's right, Aunt Rifka," Simon spoke up. "Benny doesn't want to be a farmer, but he loves animals and helps me with the chickens, right, Ben?"

Benny nodded. "And I chart the egg production every day."

"How did you learn about cows, Aunt Rifka?" asked Simon, getting back to what he needed to know.

"When I grow older, the farmer ask me do I want to help with his cows. Of course, yes, I said. This way I learned to care for cows and to make good cheese and butter. I also earn money for my passage to America. But now, boys, I am wanting to hear how you make this place a farm in so short a time."

Simon began, "Well, we started with chickens and then ducks. We still have the chickens but the ducks made so many problems that we sold them. Now we're saving to buy a cow. We'll call her Daisy."

"Daisy, is it?" Aunt Rifka said. "Already you choose your cow?"

"No, we thought maybe you could help us with that," said Simon, "but we all think Daisy would be a good name for a cow."

"*I* certainly don't," Rachel said with her nose in the air. "That name is so *common.*"

"Rachel, dear," said Mama, "it's time to do your homework." She wiped Sophie's sticky hands and began to clear away the dishes.

Later in the week, when Aunt Rifka had rested up from her voyage, Simon and Benny took her to the barn and showed her all around. "Now I feel at home, boys. Barns in Russia, they have the same smell…sweet hay and…and…"

"Old manure, right?" broke in Simon, and they all laughed.

They sat down on hay bales and Simon started in: "A farmer Benny talked to said we should buy a Jersey cow. Their milk is rich in butterfat. Is that right, Aunt Rifka?"

"Well, boys, I don't know what is a Jersey cow—but I think your farmer is right. You need cow who will give milk very rich—good for making butter and cheese."

"But we can't buy our cow yet," Simon added. "We need to get the barn ready first. And Mama and Papa said we have to wait until school lets out in June."

The sound of Mama ringing the brass bell told them it was dinnertime. Simon checked that the chickens had enough water and followed his aunt and brother in. Aunt Rifka would be a big help, he could tell.

After Mama's tasty chicken dinner, the children cleared the table. "So how were things in the old country when you left, Rifka, dear?" Papa asked.

"Things get worse and worse, I sorry to tell you. Jews, we are blamed for everything. To hear or read what some people say, we are monsters!" She sighed. "But all that the children don't want to hear, do you, children?"

Simon nodded. He wished he didn't already know.

Two short weeks after Aunt Rifka arrived, it was Passover time. Mama, Aunt Rifka, and Rachel worked from morning 'til night, making all the Passover preparations. Simon helped by handing down to Mama the special Passover dishes.

When everyone had gathered for the telling of the Passover story and for the holiday meal, Uncle Morris sat at the head of the table, with his sisters, Mama and Aunt Rifka, on either side. "I'm sure you all know this." he began. "Tonight as we pass on to our children the story of Moses leading the Israelites out of slavery in Egypt, we ask four times 'Why is this night different from all other nights?' Tonight we have a fifth answer as to why it is different: My dear sister Rifka has escaped the dangers and cruelties of life in Russia to join us in this land of freedom."

Uncle Morris pulled out a snowy white handkerchief and wiped his eyes. Simon's eyes were suddenly brimming too and he swiped at them with his napkin.

The age-old story told around the table was interesting but it seemed to last a long time, as it always did. Mama's chicken soup with matzoh balls and Aunt Rose's gefilte fish were worth waiting for, however. The evening ended with everyone singing the wonderful Passover songs.

Passover is my favorite holiday, thought Simon, and this has got to be the best Passover ever.

As the days grew warmer and the budding leaves made a soft green haze on the trees, Rifka settled in. In fact, to Simon it was hard to remember that she had arrived only a few weeks ago. With Rachel, she went to the dry goods store to pick out cloth for a dress Rachel needed. She sang Yiddish lullabies to Sophie at bedtime. She helped Mama set out dozens of strawberry plants in the garden, and she and Mama went on Tuesday nights to an English class for immigrants at the high school. They came home laughing and teasing like schoolgirls.

Best of all for Simon, Aunt Rifka told him and Benny all she knew about dairy farming. Simon had started to keep a notebook, with lists of things to do, things to buy, and things to remember. Benny kept a notebook too. His was all about money: how much they had, how much they spent, how much they needed. Aunt Rifka agreed they were good partners.

Simon loved talking to Aunt Rifka. She was such a good listener that several times he found himself on the brink of telling her about Patrick, but he held back. He didn't want her to know that the hatreds of the old country lived on in America too.

He and Patrick still pretended the other one didn't exist, but Simon noticed that Patrick hardly ever missed school and that his lunch box had more in it than bread and bacon grease sandwiches. He was curious but certainly wasn't going to ask Patrick what had changed. He just figured something good had happened to the Keegan family. One less thing to worry about, he thought.

26

Once a month, the family usually came out to visit, but now Joe came every week. One Sunday, he followed Aunt Rifka around like a puppy dog, paying no attention to anyone else. After Joe left, it was Rachel's and Simon's turn to dry the dishes. Simon carefully set down one of Mama's bone china teacups and blurted out, "I hope Joe won't make Aunt Rifka fall for him and then leave her for someone else. You remember what Uncle Herman says: 'Every time I turn around, my son has a new sweetheart.'"

"Oh, I don't know, Simon. It seemed to me that Joe hasn't been just flirting; he's beginning to fall in love," Rachel said with a dreamy look on her face.

"Well, if he does marry her, he'll be taking her away from us. Did you think of that? It would be awful. We need her to teach us about dairy farming. Besides, we love her, right?"

"Simon, you're just too young to see how romantic it is. Think about it. If they do marry, Rifka won't have to move far away. She and Joe will come out here on Sundays, like Joe does now. Aunt Rifka is so pretty that someone is sure to marry her if he doesn't. Then even if her husband didn't take her far away, she still would have to go to her husband's home for some of the holidays."

Simon thought Rachel's romantic ideas were silly, but he gave up trying to convince her how ridiculous Joe's flirting had been. Besides the flirting, Joe hadn't even wanted to go down to the brook with Simon and Benny or join the horseshoe game with the men, like he always had before. He had ruined the day—at least for Simon.

The next Sunday, Joe came early. He never left Aunt Rifka's side and stayed for dinner. He made no move to leave as Rachel and Simon cleared the table. From the kitchen Simon heard Mama say, "Joseph, if you don't leave now, you will miss the last trolley home. I know you mean well but you are wearing my sister out."

Joe didn't seem embarrassed that he had overstayed his welcome. "Hey, Simon, walk me to the trolley." Though Simon had had more than enough of Joe, he decided to go. Maybe he could talk some sense into this cousin of his.

But Joe didn't let Simon get a word in edgewise. "Your aunt is very beautiful, don't you think, Simon?" Simon just plodded along, getting madder by the minute, as Joe rattled on. "When I come out next Sunday, I'll bring her sweets from Schrafft's. They make the best chocolates in Boston."

Simon couldn't stand it anymore. "Joe, don't you see my aunt is only being polite? She'd probably love it if she never saw you again. Didn't you notice that she was pale and tired by the time you left? Besides, even a kid knows that someday soon you'll drop her like a hot potato."

"Aw, Simon, I think you're just jealous," Joe said. But he looked a bit worried and finally stopped talking.

As they approached the trolley stop, Joe said, "Seriously, Simon, do you think your Aunt Rifka wants me to stop coming?" Simon nodded his head, though he really couldn't be sure. "Go and find another pretty girl, Joe. That won't take long; they all fall for you, don't they?" Joe's smile faded. In fact, he looked miserable.

Just then the trolley came squealing to a stop and Joe climbed aboard without saying goodbye or looking back. Simon stood watching the trolley disappear around the bend. He turned to go home and for a moment he wished he'd kept quiet. But that was foolish. He could tell he'd discouraged Joe from bothering Aunt Rifka. That's what he wanted, wasn't it?

27

Though everyone expected family visitors the next two weekends, no visitors appeared. The third Sunday Uncle Herman and Aunt Bella did come, but cousin Joe wasn't with them. Simon saw Rachel take Mama aside and whisper something in her ear. Mama nodded and turned to Uncle Herman, "Where's our Joseph, Herman? The children are missing him. Is he pursuing one of his pretty young ladies?"

"Not that I know of, Eva. He's been moping around like a mooncalf for the last couple of weeks. I can't figure him out."

"Well, tell him we miss him. It's dull without him."

To Simon's surprise, Aunt Rifka added, "Me, like the children, I enjoy Yosef's mishegaas. His funny ways, they make us all laugh, don't they, children?"

Simon turned away. He had a funny feeling in his stomach. After all, he had to admit that, like Benny and Rachel, he had been bored last Sunday without Joe's antics. And like Benny, he wanted to talk to Joe about how the plan to buy a cow was coming along. Now he knew for sure that when he told Joe that Aunt Rifka hoped he would stay away, it was a lie.

In bed that night, he couldn't get comfortable.

"Golly, Simon, you're flip-flopping like a fish on a hook. Stay on your own side of the bed," Benny grumbled.

Simon made himself lie still. Poor Joe, my favorite cousin, he thought. I told him what I hoped was true, not what was really true. Sleep didn't come for a long while, not until he figured out a plan for making it up to Joe.

Simon got up early the next day so he could walk with Papa to the trolley. "Papa, would you tell Joe for me that Aunt Rifka especially said she missed him? We all do, but I think that's what I want Joe to know. After that night when he stayed so long and ignored everyone but Aunt Rifka, I told him I thought he was bothering her and I could tell it hurt his feelings."

"Oh, you did, did you? I wondered why he stayed away. It wasn't like him. Well, son, I'll give him your message."

"Papa, just one more thing: tell him I'm sorry."

"I will, son," Papa said as he climbed onto the trolley. Simon hurried home to his chickens feeling not quite so guilty.

That night, Simon met Papa at the trolley. "What did Joe say, Papa?"

Papa laughed. "He said, 'Tell Simon I'm missing all of you, too, but mostly your Aunt Rifka, I must admit.' You don't mind too much that your cousin feels that way, do you?"

"No, Papa, I just worry that Joe might make Aunt Rifka fall for him and then drop her for another girl."

"Well, son, we'll see if my nephew mends his ways. He does seem to be in love, from what I can tell." Papa put his arm around Simon's shoulder and they started home.

Sure enough, bright and early the next Sunday Joe walked jauntily into the yard. "Look, children, here's Joseph," Mama said.

Rifka put down her dishtowel and came to the door. "We all are hoping that you come. The country air, it is good for you, you know."

Joe had a big smile for Rifka, but he started out by playing ball with Simon and Benny, riding Sophie around on his shoulders, and helping Rachel pick strawberries from the garden for Mama. After he had been a good guest, he and Aunt Rifka sat on the porch swing, talking, talking,

talking. Both looked so happy that any worries Simon had about their courting were gone, as if they were shoes he'd outgrown.

The next Sunday Papa said at the breakfast table, "Benny, Uncle Herman and I have a proposition for you. We promoted Harry, our errand-boy and odd-jobs worker, so we need someone to do that job. We decided that since the summer is a slow season, we'll make this a part-time position until fall. I know you want to learn more about the business. Would you like to come in to Boston with me and work at the store two days a week?"

"Would I?" Benny squealed. "Yes, a million times! Oh, Papa!"

Uh, oh, Simon thought to himself. I was counting on Benny to help with our cow. But he knew that this job meant a step toward Benny's dream, so he made himself smile.

Papa turned to Simon. "Son, I figure you'll have your hands full with our new cow this summer, right?"

"Yes, Papa, Benny's the right one for that job."

But Benny's smile had disappeared. "There's a problem, Papa. Simon will need my help now that we're going into the dairy business."

Mama spoke up, "If the cow makes too much work for Simon, I think we could hire a boy for those two days when Benny is in the city. Mr. Fanning the grocer says he'll buy all the butter and cheese Rifka and I can make. That means we'd be able to afford a helper for those few hours."

Just then they heard a sharp knock on the door and a voice called, "Hello there." It was Mr. Benton, the farmer from the Fourth of July celebration. Simon and Benny invited him in and introduced him to Mama and Papa and Aunt Rifka. "Good day, folks. I came to talk to your sons about a cow I'm thinking of selling. Are you still interested, boys?"

"Oh, yes!" said Simon.

"A Jersey cow, if you have one," piped up Benny.

"Yes, she's a Jersey. I remember we talked about that, youngster. I thought I'd charge you thirty-five dollars. Can you manage that?"

"Oh, Mr. Benton," blurted Simon. "I heard the going rate was forty dollars. Your price is more than fair. And you came at just the right time. As soon as school is over next week, our parents say we can get our cow."

"All right, boys. Why don't you come and look at her first? If she suits you, just let me know what day next week you'll be coming to get her and I'll have my farmhand there to bring her to your place."

Simon spoke up, "Mr. Benton, is it alright if we bring our aunt with us? She knows a lot about cows. She worked in a dairy."

"That's fine, son. I can see you boys know a lot about dairy farming already, but I'm glad to hear you'll have your aunt to help as well."

With Aunt Rifka, the boys went to look at Mr. Benton's cow on Sunday. Aunt Rifka looked the pretty Jersey cow over from head to hooves. "She seem to me a healthy cow, boys. I can see she have sweet temper also. Mr. Benton is very kind man if the price is as good as you say."

As they were leaving, Simon called over his shoulder: "We'll be back to get you on Thursday, Daisy."

28

ama was waiting at the kitchen door when they came in. "Well, does Mr. Benton's cow look good?"

"Good? She's perfect," said Simon. "Isn't she, Aunt Rifka? Mr. Benton's going to lend us a wagon and driver to bring her over on Thursday. Isn't that a perfect way to start our summer vacation?"

"It surely is, boys," Mama said with a smile. "All your hard work–it is paying off now. By the way, Simon, guess who came by for you, while you were gone…your classmate Patrick."

"Patrick?" Simon stared. "What did he want?"

"I'm not sure. You know how shy he is. He looked at the floor and mumbled that he needs to talk to you. Perhaps he wants to be friends again."

Simon felt like he'd been punched in the stomach. "Well, to heck with him!" he blurted out. "Friends? I'll *never* be *his* friend again! Does he think he can say 'I'm sorry,' and I'll forget our fight and the awful things he said about Jews? Not on your life. I'm glad I wasn't here. *I'd* have been the one starting a fight this time!"

"Simon!" Mama gasped, and Simon realized that now he had told her what he had promised himself he'd never tell anyone. He twisted away so she couldn't ask questions and ran out to the barn. Did stupid Patrick think he'd forget their bloody fight and those mean, ugly words: "kike," "Christ-killer," "money-grubbing bastards"? They would never go away. Besides, he had other friends now—friends he didn't need to worry about or feel sorry for.

Simon kicked the grain bucket across the barn. How I wish I had never met Patrick and tried to help him, he raged. With his big toe throbbing, he began furiously to hammer at the stall he was repairing for Daisy.

In the midst of his banging, he heard a voice calling from the barn door: "Simon! I got to talk to you."

"Can't you see I'm busy?" he snarled, but Patrick strode right in. "If you think we can be friends again, Patrick, you can just forget it. The worst thing in my life was you jumping me and calling me those names. I never heard anyone talk like that before, ever. It was like a kick in the gut to hear that a *priest* called Jews 'dirty, greedy, money-grubbing heathens, Christ-killers," and all the rest."

"But that's what we need to talk about,' said Patrick. "I'm not saying we got to be friends. Just lemme talk." Simon sighed and turned to face Patrick. He knew he'd have to hear him out. Might as well get it over with.

Patrick started in: "When I went to confession a couple of weeks ago, I told the new priest—a young one—about the stealing and the fight and how I cussed you out."

Simon's eyes opened wide. "Holy cow, Pat. And you were so mad when I told that parks guy about what we did."

"But I had to tell my priest. I knew what I did was a sin, and in confession, you have to tell your sins. If you don't, that's another sin."

"So? I'm not your priest. Why do you want to tell me?"

"Because our new priest told me that, besides saying a hundred Hail Marys, I had to come and say I'm sorry. He doesn't believe all that about blaming Jews for killing Christ. He says Catholics who believe that are 'misguided.' That means they don't know any better. He said that Jesus was a Jew himself and we need to respect other people's religion…"

Simon couldn't take it all in. Patrick went on: "It was the old priest who told me that Jews were Christ-killers. Our new priest doesn't think that way."

"Well, that's something, I guess."

"And it wasn't any priest that said that about Jews being greedy and money-grubbers. I heard some drunk guys wobbling out of Cappy's Bar, and they were yammering about Jews."

Simon spit out the piece of straw he'd been chewing on. "So you come and apologize, just because your priest makes you do it."

"Not really." Patrick hung his head and mumbled, "It's been eating at me since our fight. I'm ashamed I said those things, if you want to know the truth. Holy heck, how many times have I heard ignorant people calling me a 'big Mick'?"

Simon remembered too. He could never forget that awful bully at school sneering and calling Patrick not just a Mick, but a big dumb Mick. And he'd seen a hundred posters for jobs that say "No Irish need apply."

Patrick continued: "And I hear people whispering with their noses in the air that we're 'shanty Irish.' So I was mad at myself for passing on the stupid things people say about Jews."

Before Simon could think of something to say, Patrick went on: "But I don't care about being friends with you. You were always feeling sorry for me and my family. I hate that. Now we don't need your pity, so there!"

Simon sputtered, "But, but..."

Patrick kept going. "My dad has a new job. He's not working at that lousy rubber factory any more. The Friends' Beans company hired him— as a crew boss. It's safer and pays better. My mother doesn't have to work now, so I can look for a summer job myself."

Simon took a deep breath. "Gee, that's great, Patrick. I *did* feel sorry about your family's problems. I couldn't help it. But if you don't want to be friends, I guess that's the way it will be." He hesitated, then plunged ahead. "I had a crazy idea that you might want to help me at our place this summer. We could use a few hours every week, and we could pay you a little." He shook his head. Did he really say that?

Patrick said nothing. He stared and shook his head. Then he said: "I give up on you a long time ago, Simon, I swear to God. On the other hand, I hear you'll be getting a cow and I know that means more work for you. And to tell the truth, I don't mind work, so long as it isn't taking care of the little kids. Boy, that Mary Catherine drives me nuts…not to mention having to change the little ones' stinky diapers…." Simon smiled. Patrick hesitated and then blurted out, "Aw, heck, we could give it a try, I guess."

When Aunt Rifka came out to call Simon for lunch, he took her to meet Patrick, who was looking Daisy's stall over. "This is my Aunt Rifka, Pat. Aunt Rifka, Patrick's going to help us with the farm work."

Simon was impressed that his aunt didn't look the least surprised but said warmly, "I'm glad to meet you, Patrick. You must be my nephew's schoolmate, yes?"

Patrick's face reddened. "Yes, ma'am," he murmured. "Pleased to meet you, ma'am." Turning to Simon, he said, "Now I got to go to the hardware store for my Pa. We're fixing that broken window today. See you next week to get those bales of hay down."

29

Simon thought Thursday would never come. And when it did, he felt too excited to eat breakfast.

Aunt Rifka came into the kitchen, pinning up her hair. "Simon, a good breakfast you'll need. Bringing your cow home, it will not be easy."

Simon got himself some oatmeal and sat beside Benny. "I don't understand why you don't want to go with us to get Daisy, Ben."

"Well, I don't, so just leave me alone."

"But why not?"

Benny sighed. "You told me Daisy just had a calf. I can't believe you're going to bring her here and leave her calf behind, that's why!"

"Benny, don't be silly. If we brought the calf, the calf would get most of Daisy's milk. Then we wouldn't have any milk to make butter and cheese to sell. We wouldn't have money to buy the hay and grain Daisy needs. And we wouldn't be earning money so Papa didn't have to work so hard. For gosh sakes, be reasonable, Benny."

"Okay, okay. I know this is what we need to do, but I don't have to see Daisy's calf bawling as you take her mother away."

Simon looked at Aunt Rifka and shrugged. She gave Benny a squeeze as they left for Farmer Benton's place.

When they reached Mr. Benton's farm, his driver led the cow out of the barn. As he tried to haul Daisy up the ramp into the wagon, she planted her feet and wouldn't budge. The driver planted *his* feet and pulled harder on the rope. The cow mooed pitifully. Her eyes rolled. Thank heaven the calf was nowhere in sight. Daisy was scared, Simon could see, and she seemed strong, too, even if she was small for a cow.

Rifka stepped forward. "No, please. Stop!"

The sweating driver growled, "But, Miss, this is the only way to get the animal into the wagon."

"Hah!" she said. "Cows I know. That is how to frighten cow. She might jump off the… What you call this, Simon?"

"The ramp."

"…the ramp. Could be break her leg. Let me…"

The driver stopped pulling, though he kept a strong hold on the halter. Aunt Rifka moved in and stroked the cow, murmuring. If the cow didn't understand Yiddish, she did seem to understand kindness. Soon she stopped pulling.

"Simon, get for me the bucket I give you, please. I try to lead Daisy up the … the ramp. You come behind so she won't jump over side, get hurt." Simon passed his aunt the bucket that held a little grain. Daisy stuck her head in the bucket and calmly followed Aunt Rifka up the ramp.

When they reached home, Daisy let Aunt Rifka lead her down the ramp and into the barn. Daisy was peacefully eating the hay Simon had forked into her new stall when Mama, Rachel, Benny, and Sophie came out to admire her.

"Mama, Aunt Rifka knew what to do to calm Daisy down. If it weren't for her, we'd still be trying to get Daisy into the wagon."

Aunt Rifka gave him a hug and got out the milking stool. The rest of the family went back to the house. It was time for a milking lesson. Aunt Rifka went first. She crooned soothing noises and showed Simon how to alternate the two front teats with the two back teats, pulling them down and then squeezing the milk out. "Be sure you grip the pail tightly with your knees. Even a gentle cow sometime might be… what you say? … nervous. A loud sound, sometime it do that. Then she kick over the bucket and all your work is for nothing."

Now it was Simon's turn. Milking isn't hard, once you get into the rhythm of it, he discovered. The quiet barn, the regular sound of the milk hitting the pail, the smell of hay calmed him down. When he stood up from the three-legged stool, his hands hurt, but the foaming pail of milk made him proud.

"My, already you make a good milker, nephew. When you finish milking, pat your cow and praise her. That sure to make her know you pleased with her."

"Thank you for all your help, Auntie Rifka," called Simon, as he carried his first pail of milk into the house. This is what I've been waiting for, he thought, with an ear-to-ear grin.

On Sunday, Cousin Joe came out, of course. The minute he arrived, Simon took him to see Daisy. "Joe, she's the best cow in the world," said Simon. She already gives us lots of milk and no trouble."

"I want to milk her. I'll bet I can do a good job."

"For gosh sakes, Joe. What do you know about milking? Besides, she's been milked this morning and won't need to be milked again until after dinner."

Joe shrugged and they both went into the house where they found Aunt Rifka stirring cabbage soup. "So, Rifka, you must be doing a good job of helping my cousin become a dairy farmer. That boy is as happy as a bee in clover."

Joe stayed all day. After the midday meal, instead of sitting around talking with Papa as he usually did, he invited Rifka for a walk. Simon heard her say, "Oh, Joe, the sun is hot. Why don't we stay here where it's cool?"

But Joe teased until she gave in. Papa and Mama didn't object, which surprised Simon.

When evening came, sure enough, Joe was still here. He went to the barn with Rifka and Simon and begged to do the milking.

"Now, Yosef, I tell you what you must know about milking," Rifka said.

"How hard can it be? I've seen people milk cows, for goodness sake."

Simon and Rifka looked at each other and shrugged. Simon thought it would be a good lesson if Daisy wouldn't let down her milk for this noisy stranger.

At first Cousin Joe looked like he'd been milking all his life. He said proudly: "Do you see how well I'm doing, dear Rifka? I'll bet no one else has gotten so much milk so fast." But as he turned toward Aunt Rifka, the legs of the stool gave a loud squeaking noise. Daisy kicked and the bucket went flying. Milk splashed everywhere, but mostly on Joe.

Aunt Rifka and Simon couldn't help laughing at Joe's red face. He looked so wet and funny. Simon headed for the house to get a towel, shaking his head. At the barn door, he paused and turned around. "Wait until I tell the family how funny you look, Joe."

But Joe wasn't paying him any attention at all. Simon watched Aunt Rifka dabbing at Joe's dripping face with a corner of her apron, and suddenly they were kissing, really kissing.

30

Simon found himself thinking a lot about that kiss. He used to think kissy stuff was silly, but after he saw Joe and Aunt Rifka kiss, he thought he might want to kiss a girl someday. Still, he was glad they hadn't seen him. He decided he wouldn't tell anyone: not Rachel, not even Benny. He'd just wait and see what happened.

Daisy provided a good distraction from all this love business. Besides being so gentle, from the beginning she gave at least two gallons of milk each day. He loved the early morning milking in the quiet barn. After he took the milk in to Mama, he led Daisy out to the field where she calmly grazed all day until the late milking. Every day he staked her in a new place, which meant he didn't have to cut the grass anymore.

He kept Daisy's stall clean, tended to the chickens, and with Benny's or Patrick's help, took over chores in the garden, which was twice as big this year. Once Daisy arrived, Aunt Rifka and Mama had lots to do in addition to the housekeeping and cooking. Aunt Rifka taught Mama how to clean all the equipment: the milking pail, the milk cans, the skimmer, the churn, and the crocks for holding the milk until the cream rose to the top. Mama and Aunt Rifka bought cheesecloth and used it to hang the sour milk curds over a bowl to drain until they turned into cottage cheese. Mr. Fanning had told Mama he'd buy for his store all the cottage cheese she wanted to sell.

Patrick turned out to be a great help on the days he came. No sooner did Simon point out rotten wood at the base of the chicken coop than Patrick appeared the next day with boards slung over his shoulder.

"I don't have to ask where those came from, do I?" Simon asked.

"Nope. From the good old dump. Now we can fix the coop before a fox gets in." Patrick helped Simon clean up Daisy's stall and then started to work on the henhouse. By the end of the afternoon, not even a garter snake could have slithered into that coop.

As they worked silently side by side, Simon realized that after the events of last winter, he never would have believed things could be so easy between him and Patrick as they were at this moment.

As if Patrick read his thoughts, he said: "Gosh, Simon, who would have thought we'd be working like this, side by side?"

"Not me, but a lot has happened, I guess."

"Yep, my dad getting a really good job changed everything for my family. When he came home and told us he'd left that lousy rubber factory to be a crew boss at the Friends plant, I thought I'd bust open, I was so proud."

"I would be too, Patrick."

They weeded a little longer in silence, when Patrick said, "Oh well, Simon, I suppose any day now, just to make things interesting, you'll have another crack-brained idea, like the swimming pool for your ducks—maybe a raft on the brook for your cow."

Simon gave him a fake punch on the shoulder and said, "I'm quitting here. We've won the battle of the weeds. C'mon in. My mother made her famous molasses cookies, and they sure taste great with Daisy's milk."

Right after breakfast the next Sunday, Joe stuck his head into the barn where Simon was milking. "Hi, Simon, how's it going?"

"Fine, Joe. Want to take a turn here?"

"No thanks. Got my courting clothes on today."

"You know what, Joe?" asked Simon as he picked up the milking stool, "You're here earlier and earlier these days. Seems sometimes like you're living here."

"Wish I could, cousin," said Joe as he headed for the house.

Simon watched him go and realized he didn't mind Joe coming so often. At least he isn't ignoring us kids any more, he thought, remembering the last time Joe came. He had played catch with them for a while, and then he'd spent time answering Benny's questions about the store.

In the weeks ahead, Joe came every weekend, except one Sunday when Rifka took the streetcar into Boston to meet him. Papa gave Rifka instructions on where to get off, but Simon found himself worrying that Joe and Rifka might have missed each other. If they did, would his aunt be all right in the big city?

When it neared time that evening for the streetcar to arrive at the Melrose stop, Simon said: "Mama, Papa, I'm going to meet Aunt Rifka's streetcar," and off he went.

He stopped worrying when he saw his aunt moving to the front of the car, smiling. When she stepped down, she hugged Simon and said: "Dear Simon, how good you are to meet me. Now I tell you all about my wonderful day." Simon wasn't very interested in the museum they visited or the fancy expensive restaurant Joe took her to.

"Sounds like Joe thinks you're very special, Aunt Rifka."

"I suppose that is true. Well, I think our Yosef, your Cousin Joe, is special also," smiled Rifka, and squeezed Simon's hand.

The next Sunday, Uncle Morris and Aunt Rose came to visit. The grown-ups sat around after lunch talking about nothing very interesting, so Simon and Benny went out to play in the brook. "Come on, Benny," Simon said when they were tired of that. "Let's ask Mama if we can walk over to Raymond's place. He has a new baseball glove."

When they came in, Simon noticed that Aunt Rifka had been crying. "Mama," he whispered, "what happened? Something sad?"

Mama laughed and Aunt Rifka beamed! Everyone else stopped talking as Mama explained: "Son, nothing sad. You remember, don't you, when I was crying for happy?"

"Yes, Mama. That was the day the letter came saying Aunt Rifka had her ticket to come to America."

"That's right, son. This is the same kind of happiness. Your Cousin Joe asked Uncle Morris and me for permission to marry your Aunt Rifka!"

Simon grinned at his cousin. "Good for you, Joe." Then he turned back to Mama, "But why did Joe ask you and Uncle Morris, Mama?"

"Well, that *is* a little sad. It's because Rifka doesn't have parents who could give their consent."

"And?" said Simon.

"And what?"

"And what did you and Uncle Morris *say*?"

"We said yes! These two are so in love and your Cousin Joe convinced us that he will be a good husband."

At that, Joe took Aunt Rifka in his arms and gave her a gentle kiss. Suddenly everyone was hugging and kissing except Sophie. She pulled at Aunt Rifka's dress, then held up her arms, crying "Up, up!" Aunt Rifka stooped and picked her up, and Joe twirled them both around, making Sophie squeal with delight.

Rachel whispered in Simon's ear: "Do you see how happy they look, Simon? Are you happy, too?"

"Of course, silly," Simon answered, "for weeks I've been rooting for good old Joe."

31

Soon after that exciting news, Mama said one evening, "I have my heart set on having the wedding in our home."

Rifka looked up from her sewing. "Oh, Eva, a home wedding I would love but you mustn't. For you it will be too much work."

"The children will all help. Right, children?"

Simon said "Right," along with Benny and Rachel, but later he remembered that question and thought: we sure didn't know what we were getting into. The wedding was nine months away, so everyone had a long time to prepare, but except for Papa hiring someone to put in electricity and getting rid of the kerosene lamps and lanterns, which he had planned to do anyway, most of the work came in the week before the May wedding. What a week that turned out to be!

Patrick came over to help Simon and Benny. Patrick hadn't been there the day Mama asked for help, but he wanted to. After all, Aunt Rifka had invited him to be a wedding guest! The boys cleaned up the barn floor and the hen house, tidied the vegetable garden, and even went after the spider-webs in Daisy's stall.

Two days before the wedding Mama asked the boys to wax the floors. Benny looked up from his Rover Boys book and pleaded. "Mama, the bad guys have Tom cornered. Let me finish the chapter. Please, please?"

"I'm sure Tom will survive, son. After the floors are waxed, you can go back to your book." Benny groaned but got up.

Mama went on: "Waxing floors is hard on the knees, boys. Pad them with these rags and it will be easier."

After a few minutes of polishing, Benny said, "This is so boring. I'm going to tie the rags on my feet. I'll skate to wax the floors and we'll be finished in no time." In two minutes, he was skating across the floor as if he were on a pond.

"That looks like fun!" called Patrick, quickly wrapping his feet with the rags and joining Benny.

Just as Simon called out "I don't think this is a good idea," Benny wailed "Ow!" and dropped to the floor. "I've got a big splinter," he wailed. "Ow, ow!" Then Patrick crashed into Benny and hit his head when he fell.

"What is all this, children?" Mama said, appearing at the door.

Benny cried, "Mama, look! I've got a splinter that hurts a lot. Can you get it out? And Patrick stumbled over me. He's got a big bump on his head."

"How could this happen waxing the floor, boys?"

"We were using the polishing cloths on our feet and skating. It's quicker," said Benny.

Mama shook her head, then took Benny's foot in her hand and teased the splinter out. "I'll bring you a cold cloth for your bump, Patrick. Was this your mischief, Simon?"

"Nope. It was mine," spoke up Benny, "Simon didn't think it was a good idea."

"Yes, I thought Simon had outgrown that kind of mishegaas. But don't you start, Benjamin." Benny nodded and sighed, Simon explained to Patrick that "mishegaas" meant craziness, and Mama returned to the kitchen where she and Rachel were hard at work preparing enough food for the forty-two guests.

The boys went back to work on their hands and knees until the floors shone like glass.

The day before the wedding, Simon's job was to pick up all the cowflaps from the lawn and the barnyard. Once he had chased Rachel with dried cowflaps and made her scream, but he thought the better of it this time. Rachel was working so hard to help Mama with all that baking.

As it turned out, he was glad he hadn't been mean to his sister. A little later, she came over to him carrying an enormous daisy chain. She and her friends often made daisy chains to wear. They would pick a lot of daisies, braid their stems together, and make garlands to wear as necklaces. Rachel seemed to be offering this huge daisy chain to him.

"Hey, Rachel, this is the longest daisy chain I've ever seen. Why are you giving it to me, for heaven's sake?"

"It's not for you; it's for Daisy. I think she should dress up for the wedding like the rest of us."

"But you didn't even want us to call her Daisy."

"You're right, I didn't. But I have to admit it suits her. Here. Take it."

So Simon took the garland for Daisy and put it away for tomorrow.

32

The next day, the wedding day, everyone was up early. "Isn't it great, Benny?" said Simon when he opened his eyes. "The sun is shining so the wedding ceremony can be outside, like Joe and Rifka wanted."

Simon went downstairs and headed out to feed the chickens. "Mama, wasn't Rachel nice to make a daisy-chain so Daisy could dress up for the wedding?"

"Yes, she told me. Now you know, son, Daisy can't come to the wedding, but you can stake your cow today beside the barn so folks can see and admire her as they arrive."

"I understand, Mama."

Guests began coming at two o'clock and many of them did admire Daisy's finery. Soon everything was ready for the ceremony. Papa had set up in the front yard under the elm tree every chair in the house and some borrowed from neighbors. Rabbi Caplan from the new synagogue in the next town was there to perform the marriage. Simon was excited. Wearing a beautiful new yarmulke on his head, he had the honor of holding up one of the poles at the corners of the chuppah. The chuppah, a beautiful fringed satin cloth, made a pretty roof over the handsome couple. Papa had explained that it symbolized the new home the bride and groom would create. Rifka, in a dazzling white dress and veil, walked around Joe seven times. Then seven blessings were said over the wine. When she threw back her veil to kiss Joe, Simon thought she had never looked more beautiful.

All the children were waiting for Joe to stamp on a wineglass that was wrapped in a napkin. Simon had explained to Patrick that this custom reminded everyone of when the Jewish temple in Jerusalem was destroyed. He knew it also meant that the world wasn't perfect and everyone must try to mend it. When Joe stamped hard and the glass shattered, a cry of "Mazel tov!" went up.

When the service ended, Simon, Benny, Rachel, and Patrick helped Mama lay out the luncheon. They were horrified when Mama said: "Now boys, you must use your best table manners today. You are not to eat until everyone else has been served, and no grabbing. Don't take anything until someone passes it to you."

Oh, no! Simon, Benny, and Patrick looked at each other in shock, but before long figured out how to obey Mama's orders without going hungry. Sitting side by side, they waited until everyone else had been served and then passed things back and forth to each other.

"Benny, wouldn't you like a piece of Mama's delicious honey cake?"

"Thank you, Simon. I don't mind if I do. How about you, Patrick?"

"It looks almost too good to eat," Patrick said, taking a big piece.

"And, Simon, these little cookies look wonderful. Help yourself."

The boys passed back and forth to their hearts' content, and since Mama didn't notice, she didn't scold a bit.

As the happy day came to an end, everyone gathered to see Rifka and Joe start off to their new home. It would be a short ride, since the house was just two miles away. Rifka had convinced Joe that after all these years apart from Mama, she couldn't bear to go very far from her sister now. "Besides," she said, "Daisy will have a new calf soon. If it's a female, that will make a second milk cow, and my sister will need my help in the dairy more than ever."

As Joe and Rifka said their goodbyes, what should come along? Not the horse and buggy everyone expected, but one of Melrose's first automobiles, a handsome Stanley Steamer, gleaming green with yellow wheels. The gentleman driving it stepped out and presented it to Joe, "Your chariot, sir," he said. Simon's mouth dropped open: "Wow, Joe, did you buy this beautiful automobile?"

"Are you kidding? No, we have it just for today."

Simon reached out his hand to stroke the shiny green door but Joe grabbed his arm. "No touching, kid. Just look." He led Rifka around and helped her into the passenger seat.

As Joe and Rifka drove off, all the grown-ups waved and called "Mazel Tov." Benny and the other excited children chased after the newlyweds. Simon resisted the fun. It was almost milking time and he didn't want Daisy to be uncomfortable.

When he turned back, he saw Uncle Herman coming out of the chicken house and heading towards Daisy. He called out: "Simon, my boy, look here. Your cow must have enjoyed her daisy chain because she's about to swallow the last few blossoms, I see."

When Simon reached him, Uncle Herman squeezed his shoulder and said: "Your old uncle can hardly believe what he sees here. Who ever would think that a city boy like you could make this place a farm in just two years? I know I laughed when you told me about your wish to be a farmer. I am not laughing today. You have taken such good care of your animals. Not many grownups would make such good farmers, I wager."

"I know before you moved out here, your Papa and Mama worried, afraid they couldn't depend on you to act sensibly, to take responsibility." Simon nodded and swallowed hard, remembering and feeling ashamed of the day Bennie fell under the horse.

"But my hat's off to you, nephew. You take all the responsibilities to your farm creatures more seriously than any of the young men at Hirsh Brothers take their work, I can tell you that."

"Thank you, Uncle Herman, but you know the farm wouldn't have happened without you and Uncle Morris lending us the money we needed. Also, this place would be just a few chickens without a lot of help from Benny and from Aunt Rifka, who knows all about dairy farming."

"Yes, I know you had help, Simon. But it was your dream. This is worth celebrating." He unwrapped one of his beloved cigars and soon was sending up great clouds of smoke.

After a few puffs, he squinted at Simon. "This has been quite a day, eh, nephew? Well, I suppose yours will be the next family celebration—next year, yes?"

Simon's stared. "You're teasing me, Uncle Herman. I don't even have a girlfriend!"

Uncle Herman nearly swallowed his cigar as he choked with laughter.

"No, nephew, not a wedding!" he cried at last. "Didn't I hear that you and your brother are studying Hebrew with the rabbi from that new synagogue in Malden? And aren't you twelve years old?"

"Oh, I see. You're thinking about when I have my Bar Mitzvah."

"That's it."

"I hope I can do it. Hebrew is hard, Uncle Herman, but Rabbi Caplan is good and Benny and I help each other. You're saying next year you'll come out from Boston to say a blessing in the service and to see if I remember my part."

Mama and Papa came over just in time to hear Uncle Herman say: "I may not need to come out from Boston to see you, Simon. If there's a synagogue next door, so to speak, this town is getting civilized. Bella has her heart set on moving out of the city and this time I think she's right. Ezra, would you try to find a house in Melrose for us?"

Mama squealed, Simon cheered, and Papa grabbed Uncle Herman in a bear hug.

Over the sounds of their excited voices, Simon heard a plaintive "Moooooo" that could mean only one thing. His cow needed him. Oh well, he knew that farmers didn't ever have a day off. He didn't mind. Daisy and the chickens could count on him. He stroked Daisy and led her into the barn to be milked.

In the quiet of that dim, sweet-smelling place, Simon could think back over what made the day so special. He was just remembering the sight of

Rifka and Joe driving away in that handsome automobile, when the barn door creaked and Patrick stuck his head in.

"Simon, you should've come with us running after Joe and Rifka. Joe took a corner too fast and ran off the road into a ditch. We all had to help push him out."

"Guess it's a good thing you chased the car. Didn't expect that you'd catch it, though, did you?"

"No, but that added to the fun," Patrick said, "Too bad you missed it." And he was gone.

As Simon picked up the bucket of foaming milk and stroked Daisy's flank, he had no regrets. He realized no day is perfect but this one came close.

Glossary

Bar Mitzvah – ceremony held in a synagogue or temple after which a 13-year-old boy takes on the responsibilities of an adult Jew

Bat Mitzvah – the same ceremony for a girl who takes on comparable responsibilities

Chuppah – wedding canopy under which the bride and groom take their marriage vows

Gefilte fish and *matzoh ball soup* – traditional foods of the Passover meal

Gelt – money

Gott tsu danken – Thank God! or God be thanked

Goy – a Gentile, or anyone who is not a Jew

Kosher – food that is ritually pure according to dietary laws of observant Jews

Landsman – someone who came from the same town or region as you in the old country

Mazel tov – literally "good luck" but "congratulations" is how it is generally used

Mishegaas – craziness

Mitzvah – a good deed

Passover or *Pesach* – the spring holiday that celebrates the escape of the Jews from Egypt. Special foods are eaten and the story of the Exodus is told so as to pass it on to the children of each generation

Shabbos – the Yiddish word for Sabbath

Shalom – peace; also used as "hello" and "good-bye"

Yarmulke – a small round cap worn by religious Jews

Yiddish – language spoken by Jews. Originated in eastern Europe and derived over the years from Hebrew, German, Polish, Russian

③ The famous wedding of Abe and Leonora Oppenheim of Brockton was held at our home in Melrose because all the Oppenheim Family Groups except Simon B Oppenheim and his family lived in Brockton, leaving 35 of the 42 guests who lived in Boston Chelsea, Cambridge and Melrose. Our house contained a tremendous kitchen with an 8 place top stove and extra large oven so big that two people could sit in front of the oven and stick their feet in the oven at the same time during the coldest days in the winter. There was no heat in the kitchen or dining room but we did have a large hot air furnace beneath the front hall cellar which had the only cellar in the house. This furnace had a hot air outlet for heat in a register beside the stairs to the up-stairs bed rooms. There were no bedrooms above the kitchen and it was covered by a solid tin roof which made plenty of noise whenever it rained. There was large back hall leading directly to the barn which was attached to the house. The had a large hay loft on top of which there was a cupola with weather vane and shutters so that person in the cupola could stand up and look outside without being seen. Besides the kitchen, back storage room and barn the house a large dining room which seated 28 for the wedding dinner and a connecting living room which seated 14 for the wedding dinner. The wedding took place across the front hall beyond the staircase to the upper floor in front of a fire place in the front parlour. We had just installed electricity before the wedding took place and had disposed of the ten kerosene lamps and two kerosene lanterns a few months before the wedding. We did not get a telephone until several years after the wedding. There were no one who had an automobile. People could take a horse drawn carriage from the near-by railroad station or walk along the sidewalk for about 6 minutes to our house. Lewis and I had been busy for several days cleaning up the barn, the storage room, the hen houses, the vegetable garden, the flower beds and the shrubbery. Mother called us together on the morning of wedding, examined us thoroughly to make sure that had bathed every part of our bodies even behind our ears which we often neglected. She gave us strict instructions for our behaviour during the wedding with emphasis on table manners. We were told not eat anything until all others had been served and were starting to eat. Then we were not grab food from the table but wait until it was passed to us. We were stunned by this edict but solved the problem by sitting side of each other and passing to our hearts content. over

Author's Note

This book had its roots in the reminiscences that Abe Segel, my husband's uncle, had of his childhood in Melrose, Massachusetts. He wrote down and shared his memories with younger family members. After reading them, I told Abe that I thought children would enjoy a book about his boyhood escapades. Abe liked the idea and wrote me more letters with additional information about growing up in the early twentieth century. I'm grateful to him for sharing with us his memories of family life, in a family that defined for me and for others who knew it the very idea of family. Abe encouraged this project. I wish he had lived to read *Duck Dreams*.

Abe's father's sudden and untimely death, when the boys were adolescents, put an end to the plans for sending Abe to agricultural college. He joined the family clothing business, but eventually was able to buy a farm and combine his love of farming with success in the business world. He and his younger brother Lou, my father-in-law, remained extremely close as business partners and best friends.

The book is fiction, however, and departs from reality in many ways. Abe was only three, not ten, at the time of the move. In the book Simon has two sisters, whereas Abe had three. However, the mean farmer who sold the boys cockerels that would never lay eggs, the ducks that climbed the bank of the swollen stream and headed for the railroad tracks, and Mama's lecture on table manners before the wedding luncheon were all straight from Abe's letters.

I believe that the move from city tenements to a nearby small town reflects an important stage of Jewish life in this country and one rarely depicted in children's books.

A nephew who read a late draft of *Duck Dreams* shared with me an interesting real life connection: an ancestor of Abe Segel owned a dairy in Lithuania and when he came to Britain in the late nineteenth century, he started a dairy in the Stanford Hill section of London. Young Simon's dream of being a farmer was perhaps in his genes!

Acknowledgments

Duck Dreams is dedicated to Abe Segel, whose memories of boyhood sparked this story.

I'm grateful to many, many others: Sally Alexander, from whose writing group I have learned so much. A noted author herself, Sally is an extraordinarily perceptive critic and teacher and a remarkable human being. I learned also from the caring and gifted members of our group as well. Librarians helped me make the book historically accurate. Any errors are my own, of course.

Family members, young and old, have helped me in one way or another, as have longtime friends Sarah Angrist and Liane Norman. Amy Kellman's encouragement is greatly appreciated. Joan Friedberg, an excellent writer, has helped me make this book better. A treasured colleague and friend, her grace and generosity have illumined my life and my work.

Finally, I owe so much to David, my beloved and loving husband, best friend and partner, a helpmate if ever there was one.